De Lancey Floyd-Jones

Letters from the Far East

Being Impressions of a Tour Around the World by Way of England, India, China, and

Japan during 1885-86

De Lancey Floyd-Jones

Letters from the Far East
Being Impressions of a Tour Around the World by Way of England, India, China, and Japan during 1885-86

ISBN/EAN: 9783337169053

Printed in Europe, USA, Canada, Australia, Japan

Cover: Foto ©Andreas Hilbeck / pixelio.de

More available books at **www.hansebooks.com**

LETTERS

FROM

THE FAR EAST

BEING IMPRESSIONS OF

A TOUR AROUND THE WORLD

BY WAY OF

ENGLAND, INDIA, CHINA, AND JAPAN

DURING 1885–86

BY

DE LANCEY FLOYD-JONES

COLONEL UNITED STATES ARMY

NEW YORK
PUBLIC SERVICE PUBLISHING CO.
1887

TO

MY BROTHER AND SISTERS,

FOR WHOSE INFORMATION

THESE LETTERS WERE MAINLY WRITTEN,

I DEDICATE THIS VOLUME.

PREFACE.

THE letters in this volume were written in the course of a tour around the world, in 1885–6, and appeared in journals of the time. They are presented now in book form, in the hope that they may interest friends and fellow travellers.

The only claim made for them is, that they give a plain narrative of the journey, and some details concerning the places of note which I visited.

DEL. F.-J.

UNQUA,
SOUTH OYSTER BAY, L. I.,
January 7th, 1887.

TABLE OF CONTENTS.

XII.

XVIII.

XIX.

XX.

XXI.

XXII.

---

* While the official title of this city is Victoria, I have called it Hong Kong, in conformity with the general practice of its residents. See page 174 for good authority.

XXIII.

XXIV.

XXV.

XXVI.

LIST OF ILLUSTRATIONS.

ERRATA.

Page 17.   For " racks," read " ricks."
Page 27.   For " stated," read " started."
Page 33.   For " Plazzo," read " Palazzo."
Page 35.   For " part," read " port."
Page 61.   For " of," read " on."
Page 64.   For " Jumma," read " Jumna."
Page 83.   For " an," read " on."
Page 97.   For " Maharana," read " Maharaja."
Page 110.   For " Bengal," read " Bombay."
Page 131.   For " related," read " selected."
Page 133.   For " matured," read " maturing."
Page 144.   For " King Oudh," read " King of Oudh."

I.

OUTWARD BOUND.

ROYAL MAIL S.S. "GERMANIC,"
AT SEA, 200 MILES FROM QUEENSTOWN,
October 16th, 1885.

A VOYAGE across the Atlantic in these days has so little of novelty about it that it's unreasonable to expect this letter to prove very interesting or entertaining. The trip is so speedily accomplished, and so many of your readers have made it, that it would be egotistical in me to assume that I could tell anything that has not been repeated over and over again; but, as this may form one of a series, I venture to send it, giving some items of the trip— particularly as I feel grateful to the good ship "Germanic," as, also, my fellow-passengers, for the pleasant days I've passed on board.

The steamer left her wharf promptly at 3.30 P. M. on October 8th, but had some little difficulty in turning her head down stream, owing to a strong tide and head wind. This was, however, after some delay, and the aid of a strong tug, effected, and we proceeded down the Bay.

There was a slight haze in the atmosphere, accompanied by occasional showers, which prevented our beautiful harbor from appearing at its best, and the passengers from seeing it to advantage ; still we enjoyed the sail, and caught an occasional expression of admiration from our trans-Atlantic friends, a number of whom we have on board. As we passed the Bartholdi pedestal, which has increased materially in height since I last saw it, I could not avoid expressing the hope that the next time I passed it, the statue of Liberty would be in place and its entire surroundings completed ; for I've always been of the impression that from its location, added to the idea it represents, it would form a grand feature of New York's superb harbor, and excite the admiration of the thousands that are to pass it in the future.

Since the above was written, both the pedestal and statue have been completed, and the result has more than equaled my expectations. The pedestal is grand ; its proportions, and general design, do great credit to the architect Mr. Richard F. Hunt, and the substantial and solid manner in which its base, together with the pedestal and the bronze statue itself have been carried up, reflects the highest credit upon its engineer, General Charles P. Stone, and will serve as a monument to his engineering skill.

Its inauguration and acceptance by the U. S. Government through President Cleveland, was attended with marked ceremonies, and numerous demonstra-

tions of military, naval and civic honors. A large delegation from the French Republic, made up of its best representatives, were invited guests and joined in the celebration. I clip from the journals of the day the impressions made on their first seeing it. On the visitors landing at Bedlow's Island, they were met by a vender of photographs of the statue and pedestal, who sang out " Souvenirs of the Statue!

" Souvenirs of the Statue! The only authentic Souvenirs! Picture on one side, words on the other."

" Very charming," said M. Bartholdi, stopping to examine them. " It is just what should have been." Then for the next half hour he was lost in admiring criticism of the statue.

" The only thing I find against it," he said, "is the wall which is too high for the porportions of the fig-ure and the statue. I'll tell you what you ought to do one of these days [to Mr. Butler]. You should grade the wall with earth, so that its height be diminished. I don't like the looks of it at present. The whole thing, however, I must say is most har-monious. It is a magnificent thing. Of course, I saw photographs of the statue and pedestal in Paris, but they gave me no idea what it looked like, be-cause the sea was not included in the pictures. Peo-ple say that the height of the Brooklyn bridge de-tracts from the height of the statue. Not at all. They don't conflict in the least. The distance be-tween them is too great for that. They are both big things, but they have nothing at all to do with one another.

"When I first came to America," said M. Bartholdi, radiantly, "I dreamed of this. I said to myself, 'What a great thing it would be for this enormous statue to be placed in the midst of such a scene of life and liberty!' My dream has been realized. I can only say that I am enchanted. This thing will live to eternity," said M. Bartholdi, looking with an expression heavenward; "when we shall have passed away, and everything living with us has moldered away."

M. de Lesseps sat on the wall surrounding the pedestal and surveyed it, keenly appreciative. "What can I say, *mon dieu!*" he asked. "I can only say that it is a triumph. It represents the progress of the two nations. It tells of liberty on these shores. Let the American people abide by its precepts." M. de Lesseps insisted upon going up among the scaffolding, and declined the least assistance. He examined everything, talked with Bartholdi, and was quite as interested in what he saw as that gentleman. Mlle. Tototte caused much anxiety to her friend and temporary chaperone, Mme. Leon Max, by scampering about in all directions. She always brought back with her the latest bulletins of the gentlemen's doings.

"It is sublime!" said M. le General de Pelissier, who went everywhere, though his wounds in the

Crimean war had made him lame. "Everything connected with this statue is impressive. I am lost in admiration of it."

"I saw the statue in Paris at the Exposition of 1878," said M. Desmons, of the Chamber of Deputies, "and I never hoped then to see it here. I can't express the honor I felt when I was asked to make the visit. It seems to me that the statue wasn't built for Bedlow's Island, but that Bedlow's Island was built for the statue."

Such were the honest impressions of its author and the honored representatives of the French nation, and I do not think it egotistical in pronouncing it one of the grandest and most imposing monuments of the world, and a credit to all connected with it; and in saying this I must not omit to mention the *New York World*, which by its zeal and voluntary use of its own columns, did so much toward arousing the spirit of all classes, to contribute to the completion of the work.

But to resume my narrative. Our pilot left us at 6 P. M., and as he stepped into his boat waved a parting salutation, adding the wish for a prosperous voyage—a sentiment that fully responded to our own feelings. We were now fairly at sea, and I began looking about to ascertain who were to be my fellow-voyagers, and learned upon inquiry, that we had a comfortable number in the first cabin (about one hundred), with something more than double that number in the steerage. A day or two later on, when the weather became fine, and after the cabin passengers had recovered from the effects of sea-sickness, I was able to make a little closer scrutiny of my companions, who I found were made up of various nationalities and professions—the English being rather in the majority. The published list shows a Member of Parliament from Scotland and his wife; the Law has its representative in one of the Queen's counsel; the English service by a major, and our own by a colonel U. S. Army and an ex-captain of the U. S. Engineers; the Press by an entertaining Irishman who represents a well-known London daily. I learned that a few of the English element had ranches in the West and are on their way to England to pass the winter with their friends, but the largest share are travelers who are returning from a hurried "run" of a few weeks in the United States, and upon questioning them I found that the greater number had been in America less than a month; and yet I've no doubt that many—even with this limited stay—thought themselves thoroughly acquainted with our people, their manners and customs, and perhaps the institutions of the Republic, and possibly some would go so far as to say they were prepared to write a book on America; the usual round being up the Hudson to Albany, thence to Niagara, and from there down the Lakes and St. Lawrence to Quebec, and so around, by the way of Boston, back to New York

city.   Some extend their journey farther westward,
reaching Chicago and St. Louis, and on their return
take in Washington and Philadelphia.   The American element on board is chiefly composed of pleasure travelers, who are to pass the winter abroad, but
there are a few bent on business, who will return
after a month or more.   Several well-established
houses of New York city and Chicago have their
buyers on board, who go out to purchase for the
coming spring styles and fashions ; and here I wish
to add that this class, who make frequent trips across
the Atlantic and have choice of the various lines, I
find give the preference to the White Star ships.

And now what shall I say of the good ship "Germanic," which has brought us so safely and comfortably across the Atlantic?   That she is one of the
very best I've had the good fortune to cross in, is
most certain.   Her complement of cabin passengers
—less than 200—is about the proper number to insure the best attendance.   The interior arrangements
are admirable.   The dining-room is amidships, and
is supplied with revolving chairs; a nicely proportioned sitting-room, just over the dining-saloon, well
lighted by side ports, and a gracefully-shaped dome
of stained glass, furnishes a most agreeable lounging
place during the day or evening.   This, as well as
every other portion of the vessel, is beautifully
lighted by the most approved mode of electric lights
of the incandescent system.   Those in the state rooms

(English cabins), are under the control of the occupant, so that he may retire at any hour, and light his room at pleasure. An immense improvement over the old system of lighting (through a lamp or candle placed in a small closet with a glass front, and connected with the cabin, but over which the inmates had no control) and how often have I, in common with many others, begged the room steward to give me a half hour's more light, that I might not retire in the dark. The present system has changed all this, and a simple thumb-screw near at hand, turned to the right or left, does it all, and lights up the cabin in the most perfect manner.

So fully am I impressed with the comfort which this light gives, that I hardly think I shall be content to cross again unless it be in a ship supplied with this improvement. Electric bells reach every part of the vessel, and not only respond to a gentle push, but are immediately answered by respectful and attentive waiters. The police of this ship is most admirable. The woodwork is constantly scoured, and the main halls and passageways—many of them covered with wood carpeting—are polished as bright as they can be made, and I never saw the kitchen table of the most dainty cook, present a cleaner or brighter appearance than the floor of the passage that leads to my state room. The table is well supplied, and the *menu* offers each day, beside all the substantial dishes, some choice articles of game, and oysters on

the half-shell are given at nearly every lunch. All
dishes are served after the French style, and the food
generally comes to the table piping hot.

The voyage has been a rough one, especially so
for this season ; still, our good ship has averaged
about 330 miles daily, and has made the passage
across in eight days and eight hours ; but so comfortable have we been that I, in common with many
others, almost regret that the voyage is so near at
an end.

Queenstown, October 17th, 7 A. M.—We touched at
this beautiful harbor at an early hour this morning,
and the anchor was let fall just as the sun was making its appearance in the horizon. The shores were
near at hand—so near that we could see distinctly the
stone walls which separate the various fields, as, also
the sheep and cattle that were scattered through
them—but the town was some miles away, and we
could only catch a glimpse of some parts of it in the
far distance. To save time, the steamers of this,
"The White Star Line," as well as most others, are
met near the entrance of Queenstown, by steam-
tenders that take off the English mails and passengers bound for Ireland. Quite a number of steerage,
but only two or three cabin passengers disembarked
here. This was speedily accomplished, and we were
soon again steaming away up St. George's Channel,
with our prow toward Liverpool. I observed, as
we passed along, that the shores presented a much

grayer appearance than I'd ever before seen in Ireland. This was new to me, as I never before approached the Emerald Isle without finding its verdure almost perfect, and the grass a beautiful rich green, that reminded me of spring in America.

This I was told, was due in a measure to the stubble fields—most of the oat crop having been recently gathered—but is mainly owing to the very dry season, which has been unprecedented throughout many parts of Ireland.

We have still nearly two hundred and forty miles to make before reaching Liverpool, but, as our voyage is practically over, I bring my letter to a close. You may hear from me again somewhere in England; till then I say *au revoir*.

II

LIVERPOOL TO LONDON.

REGENT HOTEL,
ROYAL LEAMINGTON SPA, ENGLAND.
October 22d, 1885.

MY last closed on October 17th, as we were steaming through the Irish Sea, with our prow pointed towards Liverpool. We were not lucky in regard to the tide, and when the "Germanic" reached the bar of the Mersey river, at 10 o'clock P. M., it was found it could not be crossed 'till the following morning — hence we anchored for the night. I, not being among the impatient ones, rather liked the idea of sailing up the river in broad daylight, than of arriving in pitch-darkness. We were under weigh again about 7 A. M. the following morning and steamed rapidly up the twelve miles that intervene between the bar and the city.

The fairly-observing American traveler who enters for the first time the Port of Liverpool will naturally be on the lookout for that forest of masts which he is accustomed to see along the piers of New York city and other commercial ports, and, not finding it, would with reason exclaim, " Where is that immense fleet of vessels that I observe daily reported as entering and departing from this port? Surely, they have not hidden them away, and yet I see only a straggling vessel or two in the river." A little closer observation, and by looking over the roofs of the warehouses which line the river front of the city, will enable him to see the topmasts and upper spars of the ships he is looking for, and this again begets the question, " What are they doing there, away up in the city? Why not leave them in the river and along piers, as in all the seaport cities of the United States?"

The answer to this calls up the superb dock system of Liverpool—one that has been in existence for very many years and is contemporary with its earliest existence as an extensive commercial port. The tides, which with us do not have usually a rise or fall of over three feet, at Liverpool rise and fall 21, and the springtides even 26 feet ; the consequence is that the river front of the city at low water is almost bare, and vessels that anchor in midstream must necessarily be a long way from the warehouses, necessitating expensive lightering in discharging and receiving cargo, beside being exposed to accident from storms while lying in the river. It was to obviate this that the dock system was introduced, and although made in the most substantial manner and at great expense, yet the convenience it offers renders it most attractive to the average shipmaster and owner, in spite of the dues which it entails.

I passed two days in Liverpool, one of which I devoted to the examination of its beautiful docks, and without entering into the minute details of their construction, I will simply state that excavations are made along the river front, and the basins thus formed surrounded by massive walls and quays, with lock gates on the river front. These, at high tide, are opened by hydraulic power, and the water admitted, and with it the vessels. When the tide ebbs the gates are closed—the pressure from the water in the basins keeping them almost water-tight. These various basins are connected by interior locks, which increase the berthing space, and add to their efficiency. Along the borders of these docks are constructed the warehouses and sheds, in which are stored the various cargoes while awaiting shipment or transportation to the interior. In many instances railway tracks connect them with the main lines of roads, thus materially reducing the expense of drayage. The docks cover an immense space—the area on the Liverpool side being 1,000 acres, while that at Birkenhead (the Brooklyn of Liverpool) is about 500, making an aggregate of over 1,500 acres. Besides this style of dock there are immense " graving docks " (we call them " dry docks "), built of massive masonry, provided with every convenience and able to accommodate the largest class of vessels. While making the tour of these docks, which I did in company with the intelligent agent of the Atlantic Mutual Insurance Company, I did not fail to remark upon the large number of vessels that were lying idle, and among them some old favorites of mine, in which I had made voyages across the Atlantic. I was told the number of vessels lying up for want of employment was still greater at Birkenhead—a substantial proof of hard times in the shipping interest. These docks have been constructed at various periods, and usually bear the names of the distinguished person who opened them to the public. The " Princess" Dock is the one near which is the landing stage, where most of the travelers to or from America embark or land. Then there are " The George," "Nelson," " Trafalgar," "Wellington," "Victoria," " Albert," and one of the latest bears the name of the Crown Princess, Alexandra, who assisted at its opening ; and a magnificent dock it is, extensive in area (covering 44 acres), with 12,000 feet of berthing space, and surrounded with most massive quays, on which are the neatest and most convenient of brick warehouses, giving the impression, like its lovely and graceful sponsor, of something fair to look upon. When I passed it the Oregon was lying in its basin, being refitted preparatory to resuming her place as a passenger ship in the Cunard line, after six months in naval service as a fast cruiser. I believe the only work she did was to carry some distinguished naval commander to the Irish coast. While upon the subject of docks and shipping, it may not be out of place to correct the impression which obtains among many Americans, that the English trans-Atlantic lines are the largest in point of tonnage in the world ; such, however, is not a fact. The first being the Peninsular and Oriental Company, which has 51 steamers and trades to the far East ; the next is the French Trans-Atlantic, which in addition to its line to this country has a large fleet trading to South America and the West Indies. Then comes the British India, whose commerce is with the East Indies and Australia ; then, I believe, follows the Austrian Lloyds.

While wandering along the quays and looking through the large warehouses I did not fail to remark upon the superb dray horses with which Liverpool abounds. I stopped and questioned the driver of a very fine team, and learned that his animals averaged 18 hundred each—112 pounds to the hundred weight. He told me that the largest dray horse he had known weighed 22 hundred—2,464 pounds. A share of these animals are raised in the neighborhood, but a goodly number come from Wales and about York, and from the Clyde district. From this fact, I believe, they are often called Clydesdale horses. Many of the best cost from $500 upward. Most of the teams were composed of two horses, driven tandem before tip carts with very broad beds and high sides, capable of containing immense loads.

Not being in any great haste to reach London, as so many of my fellow-passengers were—most of them having left by the earliest train—I decided to reach it by easy stages and not miss the beautiful country which lies between Liverpool and the great metropolis. I also wished to take in some places never before visited, and accordingly fixed upon this beautiful section of England, generally regarded as one of the most attractive portions of the entire kingdom, not alone from its great productiveness, fine parks and forests, but also from its proximity to such historical points as Kennilworth, Warwick Castle, Stoneleigh Abbey, Coventry, etc. These places are all within easy drives of Leamington, and through a beautifully picturesque country.

For leaving Liverpool I chose a rapid train of the North Western Line, one of the best managed in the kingdom, and which runs some of its fast trains at the rate of 45 miles per hour.

Being early at the station, I had a good opportunity of inspecting the train, which was made up of saloon carriages and which were connected by an odd contrivance, a species of bellows door-way, through which the occupants could pass from one to the other, this leather bellows arrangement admitting the play necessary between carriages, when the train was moving rapidly. I chose one of the former, and found it exceedingly comfortable—hardly as much so as the Pullman drawing-room car, but still very easy, nicely upholstered, and provided with very complete toilet arrangements, and a connecting smoking-apartment. The main line of this road runs through a very fertile district, very attractive to the agriculturist—but hardly as varied and picturesque as that of the Great Western — passing such well-known places as Crewe, Stafford, Litchfield and Rugby. The day was rather dark and grey, so that the view from the car windows was not as attractive as I've sometimes found it ; still, I took great pleasure in watching the highly-cultivated fields, the well-kept thorn hedges, which enclose them, and the heavy crops of potatoes, turnips and beets, which were being gathered. The beautifully-proportioned racks of hay and grain— nearly all protected by a neatly-thatched covering that must have cost no little labor and skill—were my especial admiration, and ever have been on former visits. At Rugby I changed trains and came to this place. I had time to get a very comfortable lunch at that point and was reminded of its famous school by one of its pupils, who met his father at the station.

I am comfortably lodged at this hotel and have one of the tallest of four-post bedsteads, with the cleanest of linen sheets on it, in my apartment.

What I saw here and in the vicinity I must reserve for a future letter.

III.

ENGLISH COUNTRY LIFE.

HOTEL METROPOLE, LONDON, ENGLAND.
November 5th, 1885.

I MAILED my last from Leamington, in Warwickshire, one of the finest counties of England —not only at the present time, but evidently so in the past, as within its limits some of the most noted castles and baronial residences of former days were located, as also, some of the most interesting and important events in English history have transpired.

As soon as practicable, after securing my room at the " Hotel Regent," which is located on a broad street called " The Parade," I made arrangements with the landlord for an open Victoria, to drive about the surrounding country, wishing to avail myself of the fine weather then prevailing, knowing how speedily the clouds gather at this season of the year, and how quickly sunshine is followed by rain. Driving up " The Parade"—the principal thoroughfare and site of the larger shops—we were soon in the suburbs of the town, where are situated the handsome villas

which form the residences of its best citizens, and of
visitors, who occupy them for some months, and of
some wealthy Manchester merchants, who make
their homes here. Leamington being quite a hunting centre, these villas are sought for by that class,
and I was told that three or four Americans, fond of
the chase, lived here during the hunting season.

Turning to the right, after leaving "The Parade,"
we entered the Lillington road, and drove past the
"Midland Oak," said to be as near as possible in the
centre of England, but whether this means territor-
ially or geographically, I could not ascertain, and I
discussed the matter with an officer of the Royal
Engineers.

A drive of two or three miles further along a
beautiful macadamized road, bordered by well-tilled
fields, brought us to the entrance of Stoneleigh Park.
A pretty porter's lodge guards the entrance, and a
neatly-dressed matron opened the gate. After passing some fine old beech, chestnut and elm trees, we
came upon what remains of the Abbey—a brick
structure, highly picturesque, from being nearly overgrown with ivy. Beyond this is the present family
residence—a fine large mansion of stone in the Cor-
inthian style, located near the Avon, with its grounds
handsomely terraced down to the river. The family
being in residence, admission could not be obtained,
but I was informed that there were some interesting
portraits in its various apartments. Continuing the

drive through Leigh Park and estate, which must cover several thousand acres, we crossed the Avon river by a pretty bridge, and then passed into the shooting preserves, where we saw large numbers of pheasants and rabbits. It being near sunset they were out feeding, and many crossed the road in front of us. I was told there was also a deer park, but we did not pass it. The portion of the drive through the shooting preserve is beautiful. Large trees border the road, and, in many instances, interlace overhead.

From Leigh Park we continued on to Kenilworth Castle, which is in ruins, but a grand old ruin it is. I wandered for a time through the most notable remains, such as " Cæsar's Tower," " Great Hall," " Leicester Buildings," " The Kitchens " and "Strong Tower." In the latter, Sir Walter Scott locates the prison of "Amy Robsart," Countess of Leicester. I returned to the carriage and drove back by a more direct route to Leamington, making in all, a drive of about twelve miles. In the course of this trip, I had a fine opportunity of observing the autumn foliage of England, which is more striking than I imagined. While the deep, rich tints of some of our forest trees, such as the swamp and soft maples and the like, are wanting, yet the general effect produced by a large park or forest of trees in their autumn dress, is fine. The beech, of which there are many fine specimens, has the most pronounced coloring—a deep, reddish-brown that contrasts well with the delicate yellow of the chestnut. One passes, too, fine specimens of the holly, covered with the richest of red berries.

My attention was called to some of the rookeries, usually a clump of trees apart from the main forest, where the rooks assemble and nest. This bird is one of the pets of the farmer, as also the country gentleman, who take great pride in them, and are careful to see that they are protected. I was told that when the birds become numerous, they quarrel frightfully, and the result will be a general scattering of the colony, unless their numbers are reduced ; this can only be done by a long-range rifle, when the rooks are full grown, as the bird is a shy one. He resembles, in many particulars, the crow of our country, and only a close observer would detect any material difference. The most noticeable thing I saw was his size, which is considerably less than our bird, and a whitish color about the base of the beak. Another difference, that I was told of, was that the rook never feeds upon carrion, or decomposed flesh, but he is of great service to the farmer by reason of the number of slugs he destroys. We saw also a number of skylarks, but at this season that bird soars but a short distance in the air and his song is faint.

I returned to the Regent Hotel in time for an excellent six o'clock dinner, and I will add, for the information of your readers, that the cost of the victoria, single horse with driver, for the afternoon, was $3.00, and I supplement this with a day's charges at

that well-kept hotel, regarded as the best in Leamington.

	Shillings.	Pence.
Apartments................	3	0
Attendance......	1	6
Dinner...	5	0
Breakfast	3	0
Lunch..................	2	0
Total.................,..........	14	6—about $3.50.

I was advised by the landlord that board by the
week would be furnished at the rate of $2.62 a day,
not high figures for one of the best hotels in an attractive watering place.   By referring to the guide
book, I found that the Leamington Spa has a very
considerable celebrity, and its saline waters are
claimed to be efficacious in cases of gout and rheuma-
tism. " The Royal Pump Rooms" and baths are
most conveniently fitted up, and have handsome
gardens attached, where visitors may pass their
time. Altogether, my impressions of the town
and its vicinity are most agreeable, and I'm quite
sure of wandering back there some day.

My next excursion was to Warwick Castle, which
is but two miles from Leamington, and easily reached
by tram car—a very considerable saving of expense,
as I believe the fare was only six cents. Warwick
Castle is one of the most interesting, as also one of
the best-preserved, of the baronial residences in the
United Kingdom. A recent regulation of its present
owner renders it accessible nearly every day of the
week. A fee of twenty-five cents is exacted from

each visitor, but for this you have intelligent guides to conduct you through its various halls and apartments and the adjoining grounds. The Castle is reached by a roadway, cut out of the solid rock, and with handsome trees bordering the drive. You cross the moat (now dry,) by a drawbridge, with its portcullis still in place, and enter the interior. Immediately opposite, as you enter, are two fine towers, used in former days as defences for the place—the guard rooms being in the upper stories, and commanding a view of the exterior country. From the top, I saw one of the finest parks in England, and in the far distance Edgehill, where Cromwell fought one of his important battles. The prison of the Castle, which I visited, is in the basement of one of these towers, and is a dark, gloomy-looking place.

From the interior court you enter the main apartments. A neat, gothic portico protects the entrance. The first to which you are conducted is the " Great Hall," a handsomely-proportioned room of about 60 feet in length, 40 feet in width, and 25 in height. It has an immense open fire-place, a heavy oak ceiling in panels, marble floor, and its walls are wainscotted in oak to a considerable height Four superb pairs of antlers of the Irish elk, dug up from the bogs of Ireland, adorn its walls, or as our guide expressed it, "Those are four pairs of h'antlers of the h'Irish h'elk from the bogs of h'Ireland."

The objects of interest in this grand banqueting

hall are numerous. Several suits of armor, belonging
to different periods, are arranged on one side. Cromwell's helmet and a Puritan hat in iron are among the
curiosities. Guy's punch-bowl, capable of containing
over 100 gallons, and several handsomely-carved
pieces of furniture in oak, are also on exhibition. I
was greatly impressed with this room, and admired
its fine proportions. The views, from its windows,
of the river Avon and the park beyond were superb.
The water here, being of considerable depth, formed
one of the defenses of this side of the place, while a
high crenelated wall, with an interior banquette, furnished, with the towers, the defenses of the other sides.

From the banqueting hall we were taken through
several other apartments, such as the red drawing-
room (or ante-room), the cedar drawing-room, gilt
drawing-room, state bed-room, chapel, etc. In all
of them were more or less historical portraits by
the old masters. After this we visited the gardens
and the greenhouse, where the Warwick vase, an
antique dug up near Adrian's villa, at Tivoli, is placed.
It is a superb specimen of ancient art, and the largest
marble vase extant. Its fine proportions and graceful decorations have been the admiration of all who
have visited it. I finished my day's work at Warwick, by visiting Lord Leicester's Hospital and St.
Mary's Church, a very old structure, containing several objects of interest, and where lie the remains of
Robert Dudley, Earl of Leicester. Then, after a

simple lunch at the railway station, I took an express
train for London, passing by Banbury and Oxford,
and came at once to this large and convenient hotel,
where I've been more comfortable than ever before
in England. It is superbly built and finely decorated and furnished. The lower floor is taken up with
the vestibule, and offices, dining rooms, reception
room, library and salon, which are as fine as any
thing I've ever seen. Over $5,000,000 have been ex-
pended in its construction alone.. Its prices are not
high, and one lives very comfortably for about $4.50
per day. I've done very little sight-seeing in London,
but have availed myself of the hospitality of some
friends to visit them at their country seats—especially General Sir Frederick Fitz-Wygram, in Hamp-
shire, and Mr. Edmund S. Hanbury, in Hertfordshire. The English are very fond of their country
homes. It is there they collect their household
treasures, and the living at a well-conducted English
place is almost perfection.

In this connection, it seems quite appropriate to
give my experience at one of these handsome houses,
as described in a letter written in the autumn of '81.
My brother and self were enjoying at that time the
sights of London, when we received a note asking us
to pass Saturday and Sunday at Bedwell Park, an
old country seat in Hertfordshire, England ; an invitation which we gladly accepted.

We were fortunate in our visit to Bedwell Park as

the country was looking particularly fine. The late
autumn rains having given a freshness to the entire
vegetable world that was particularly pleasing and I
never saw English turf wear a brighter green.
Taking the 3 p. m. train from King's Cross station,
London, we were about an hour by the Great Northern Railway making the journey to Potter's Bar,
the usual railway station of the residents of Bedwell
Park. Here we were met by our kind host and
his charming wife, who had also just come from
London.

After the usual salutations we were invited to
enter the carriages that were in waiting ; my brother
being asked to take a seat in the phaeton with
madam, who drove a pair of spirited blacks, while I
followed with Mr. H——y, in his dog cart.

The drive of five miles was delightful, the road
passing through a highly cultivated country, and, at
times, through avenues of superb beech and oak trees
which were in full leaf, although turned by recent
frosts. The entrance to the park is marked by a
handsome gate and porter's lodge, and, as we passed
through, a kindly bow and pleasant smile from the
porteress assured us we were welcome. The road
that leads up to the residence is lined with some superb trees, evidently of great age and probably
placed there by some of its earliest residents. We
were asked immediately on our arrival to the library,
a large and handsome room, overlooking the lawn,

and, soon after, the usual five o'clock tea, with the accompaniment of brown bread and butter was served. This custom of offering tea at this hour is quite general throughout England, and is not confined to country homes. The city residents also observe it, and in the London season the lady of the house will generally be found at home at that hour, after which driving or walking is in order, until time to return and dress for dinner, usually about 7:30 P. M.

Our walk on this occasion was through one of the handsome groves of the park, a portion of which was wild and filled with thick underbrush, a safe place of retreat for the various species of game that we stated on the way. Among them were pheasants, partridges, rabbits and hares. As we were returning home, the cock-pheasants were settling themselves for the night in the branches of some of the large oaks, and I observed that they uttered a cackling sound. This my hostess told me was intended as a warning to the flock of their roosting place—a most indiscreet measure as the poachers can mark the trees, and at night make sure of their prey. We had seen, in various parts of England, evidences of certain methods to prevent the poacher from exercising his unlawful practices, such as dotting the fields with branches of the thorn tree which prevents his using his nets successfully in catching partridges.

On our way back to the house we passed through the vegetable garden, which was in excellent condition, and filled with every variety pertaining to the climate of England.   We also visited the hot houses, graperies and fruit houses.   In the former we saw the cantaloupe melon growing upon trellis work, each melon being supported by a bracket or hanging basket.   I mention this as showing at what great expense this fruit is raised in England, and how limited must be the number that can indulge their taste for it.   We reached home, from our brisk walk of more than an hour, in time to dress for dinner and feeling all the better for the exercise.   The gong gave us warning of the dinner-hour.   By-the-by, this fashion of announcing the hour of breakfast and dinner by the Chinese gong is quite general throughout England, and its propriety becomes very apparent when one is lodged in a house of forty or fifty rooms.   Scarcely any other method could make the guest aware of the hour, as English houses are not, like French ones, liberally supplied with clocks. Dinner was served mainly in the French style, with the exception of one or two dishes which were carved by the host and hostess.   The three men servants who attended at table, performed their duties, and moved about so noislessly that their presence was hardly perceived, and to my taste, there are no better trained nor more expert servants than one finds in a well regulated English home.

We retired quite early, and our day of active work secured for us a sound and refreshing sleep.

We were roused in time to join the family in prayers, a few minutes before nine, at which service nearly the entire household assembled—at least all that could be spared; and as there were eighteen servants in this establishment, exclusive of some employed about the stables, the congregation was quite respectable in numbers. Mrs. H——y kindly gave me some items relative to her household that may be interesting to Long Island housekeepers. Servants' wages vary, of course somewhat, but she usually gave her cook $200 per annum, for which compensation she was expected to cook meats, game and vegetables well, and also supply the necessary desserts, and with her assistant cook, for the servants who have an entirely different character of table. Housemaids receive from $100 to $150 per annum. All get a certain allowance of beer or porter. Domestics that wish to give up their situations are required to give one month's notice of their intention, and, on the other hand, the mistress of the house, if intending to discharge any in her employ, is compelled to notify them one month in advance. But changes of this nature are far from being as frequent as with us, and servants often continue many years in the same family.

An English breakfast is usually a very informal meal, the guests taking their seats at table, irrespective of those they occupied at the more formal one of dinner, and after the tea and coffee is served, the waiters generally retire. Cold meats and game usually are to be found on a side table, and if one wishes them he helps himself. This strikes an American rather oddly at first, but one soon gets accustomed to it. If the post has arrived the letters and papers are brought in, and any one is free to read them if they will, and it gives the host and hostess of a large establishment an opportunity of attending to their correspondence early in the day and to send replies by the first mail.

After breakfast we made quite a thorough inspection of the interior of the house, and also surveyed it from its exterior. It is not an easy matter for me to describe Bedwell Park Mansion House, especially to the well instructed architect, as it does not belong to any of the well established orders. It is a long, rather low, rambling pile of brick, which appears to have grown at different periods—portions of it dateing back 200 years—and it evidently resembles the residences of that date. A central tower over the main entrance is one of its most prominent features and others of less height are at each end.

The grounds immediately adjoining the house are terraced and laid out in the Italian villa style, and are in beautiful condition. The number of rooms would be rather startling to an American house-wife. I counted twenty-seven on the second floor alone. Those of the first floor are not so numerous, but are larger. The salon, or drawing room, is 75 by 35 feet with proportional height of ceiling, and is a very handsome and well proportioned one. Its walls are covered with pictures, many by the best masters. I noticed two Murrillos, a Rembrandt, one or two by Rubens and a Van Dyck. There are also several portraits of the Eardley family from whom this valuable property of about 800 acres descended. The furniture of the salon I observed was, in its general character, of the style of Louis XIV. The library is a large room much used by the family, and an inspection of its shelves showed that the collection of works was not only extensive, but very choice.

One of the noticeable features of this establishment, is that of keeping a daily register of the occupants of the sleeping apartments ; and I observed too, it was in the hand writing of the lady of the house. All the rooms are numbered and those of the register correspond with those on the doors. Our host also asked us to record our names in a book kept for the purpose, a practice adopted by his father, who occupied this mansion many years, and which has been continued since his death. As time passes on this will certainly become a most interesting volume for him and his descendants.

As Sunday was included in our visit, we attended the parish church, only a short walk from the Mansion House. We found a very old building, with its interior arranged with high backed square pews. Our host and family occupying the one on the right of the pulpit, while another family of the gentry filled the one on the opposite side.

The pastor gave us a good, sensible discourse, and the congregation, made up chiefly of the villagers and farmers of the neighborhood, took an active part in the services, Among the drives we took in the neighborhood was one to Hatfield House, the residence of the Marquis of Salisbury. We were disappointed in not seeing its interior. More than 200 years ago it was a royal residence, and during the latter part of the reign of Queen Mary, Elizabeth lived there as a sort of prisoner. The old oak tree, under which it is said she was sitting when she received the news of the death of Queen Mary and her accession to the throne, is carefully protected by an iron fence.

The grounds of Hatfield House are beautifully laid out, and numerous avenues of fine old oaks and linden trees lead from it in various directions, furnishing most attractive drives, to which the general public have access. We saw immense numbers of pheasants, and other varieties of game, while driving through the estate, but was told the Marquis cared little for sport of this nature—his taste being for political distinction, which he has certainly attained.

IV.

LONDON TO THE ADRIATIC.

ROYAL HOTEL, DANIELI,
FORMERLY PLAZZO BERNARDO, VENICE, ITALY.
December 2d, 1885.

THE above caption gives the locality from which I write, and will convey to your readers some idea of the nature of the buildings which furnish the hotels for the modern traveler. The hotels, "l'Europe," "Grand Britannia," and " Grand Hotel"—all located on the Grand Canal—were formerly residences of the grandees of this quaint and fascinating old city. It is seventeen years since I was last here —time sufficient, in America, to bring about many changes, but I discover scarcely any. The gondolas —about 3,000 in number—have the same sombre appearance externally, and are as comfortable and fascinating internally, as then. A row in one of them upon the Grand Canal of a bright sunny day like the present, with palaces on either hand, is as charming as I found it in the month of May, 1868. Byron's description of them, as given in " Beppo," appears to me so thorough and accurate that I cannot refrain from quoting it:

> " Didst ever see a gondola?   For fear
>   You should not, I'll describe it you exactly :
> 'Tis a long, covered boat that's common here ;
>   Carved at the prow, built lightly, but compactly;
> Row'd by two rowers, each called gondolier,
>   It glides along the water looking blackly—
> Just like a coffin clap't in a canoe;
>   Where none can make out what you say or do.
>
> And up and down the long canals they go,
>   And under the Rialto shoot along ;
> By night and day, all paces, swift or slow ;
>   And round the theatres a sable throng,
> They wait in their dusk livery of woe :
>   But not to them do woeful things belong,
> For sometimes they contain a deal of fun,
> Like mourning coaches when the funeral's done."

I add for your information the fact, that under the Venetian Republic the extravagance exhibited in the decoration of these gondolas called forth an edict of the Government requiring that they should be painted black and their furnishings be of the same color, from which there has been no change.   Steam has, however, intruded itself even here, and a line of small ferry boats now shoot under the arches where Shylock, the Jew, loaned the 3,000 ducats to Antonio.   Only fifty years since the far-named Rialto was still an important place to the money changers and dealers in gold fabrics, but its glory and importance has departed, and as I passed by this afternoon I saw only a few poor tenants with the most inferior wares on sale.

But I am getting in advance of my journey, and must turn back and tell of the trip from London to the Adriatic.   It is by no means a short one, yet I accomplished it with very considerable comfort, quite leisurely and with no little interest.   That portion of the journey between London and Paris is now made in eight hours.   They have increased the speed on the rail lines, and added to this is a material improvement in the harbor of Boulogne; hence a larger and finer class of steamers now run between Folkstone and that part in France.   Leaving London at 9.40 A. M. by the South Eastern Railway, no stop is made between it and Folkstone.   The crossing to Boulogne is accomplished in something more than an hour, and the run from there to Paris is made in four hours.   This service is now a fixed one and no longer dependent, as formerly on the tides.   I can't say that the journey is cheap, costing, as it does, first-class, $15 ; and while on the subject of fares I will add that those of all the rail lines, both in England and on the Continent, seem very high to us.   The distance between Paris and Venice is 730 miles ; time, 32 hours ; fare, first-class, $30—something more than four cents per mile ; and when one selects such a luxury as a sleeping car a round sum is exacted.   The following is my bill for less than twelve hours in a sleeper between Paris and Basle, occupying only a single berth:

	Francs.
Sleeping car ticket	21.00
Tax for purchasing in advance	1.75
Government tax on each ticket	4.50
Stamp	0.10
Total	27.35

Or about $5.47—figures rather startling to the average American and rather disposing him to travel only by day, as hotel prices for an entire day are usually less. All this comes from the great monopolies that exist here, as, also, the high Government tax. We would regard in America such figures as almost prohibitive and the Pullman Company, with such charges, would soon be forced into bankruptcy from lack of travel. Baggage, too—which, by the by, becomes "luggage" as soon as it crosses the Atantic—is also an expensive luxury. My trunk, weighing about 100 pounds, cost, between Paris and Venice, $4.50—neither Switzerland nor Italy allowing any free baggage; only a moderate-sized hand-bag is allowed in the carriage with each passenger.

Of course, I passed some time in Paris. All good Americans find it an attractive city, but possibly less so than formerly Having a number of friends there, I mingled quite a good deal in the American Colony, and I think they all agreed that Paris was losing many of its former attractions and that there were now fewer permanent residents. On the other hand, England is gaining in this respect, and one hears of Americans renting houses by the year. The natural inference is that they like it better and are cordially received in society, where they mingle freely with the best intelligence of the country.

Thanksgiving day was observed in Paris by a good

share of the American residents attending church in the morning and a family gathering in the evening. I was fortunate in having an invite to the home of my friend, Mr. Charles J. Cl——h, who has a charming family and a most delightful apartment on the Avenue d'Jena, near the " Arc de Triompe," one of the best quarters of the city. Among the numerous tempting dishes that were served our "national bird" was conspicuous, Of course, we drank to sweethearts, wives and absent friends. It was a late hour when the party broke up.

I found Paris exceedingly neat and clean—at least it was so in the parts I visited. The streets are in admirable condition, and many are now paved with wood—this having been laid down within the past three years. It seems to stand the heavy traffic well, as I saw no holes or broken places ; but it remains to be seen if this style of pavement lasts. It seems, however, to be a success in London, where it has been down some years longer.

Coming from Paris to this city one has a choice of routes. He may reach here either by way of the Mont-Cenis Tunnel, which route passes through Macon, Aix-les-bains and Modene, Turin and Milan, or by the St. Gothard Tunnel, which takes you by Basle, Lucerne, Bellinzona and Milan. I chose the latter, as being to me the most novel and furnishing the finest scenery. The journey of that section of the road running from Paris to Basle, in Switzerland,

was made at night, as the country, especially at this
season, is not particularly attractive. We breakfasted at the capital of. Switzerland at an early hour,
and then continued on towards Lucerne—the country growing more and more attractive ; from Lucerne
the scenery becomes grand. The line follows the
border of the lake for some distance and then plunges
into the gorge of the river Reuss. From this point
on, the views are superb and the engineering skill
shown in the construction of the road excites our
admiration. At times we could see the track both
above and below us, so rapid is the ascent. The
tops of the higher peaks were covered with snow,
and the day being rather mild, the melted snows
formed pretty cascades that streaked the mountain
sides, churned into foamy whiteness through their
successive leaps from cliff to cliff. We dined at
Goschenen at one o'clock and immediately after
entered the Grand Tunnel—the longest in the world,
measuring ten miles, which we made in twenty-three
minutes—good work considering the rapid rise that
is made in passing through it. At its highest point
my pocket aneroid barometer marked about 4,000
feet. We came out of the tunnel at Ariola, at which
place the waters flow towards the Adriatic. The
descent by the Italian side is less abrupt and. fewer
tunnels were necessary in the construction of this
portion of the work. We arrived at Milan on time
and quite ready to enjoy the real comforts of the

famous "Hotel de la Ville," one of the very best in Italy. Fog prevailed during the day and a half I could spare for Milan, and to some degree destroyed the external effect of its famous cathedral ; but I passed some hours wandering through its massive interior and inspecting its various monuments and tombs.

I have been most comfortable during the two days passed in this quaint and unique old town. My room faces the harbor—and the entrance of the Grand Canal, and, as we have had the brightest of skies, Venice has appeared at its best. The gondolas have been in their summer dress and apparently all brought out from their hiding places, as I counted this morning seventy-five just in front of my balcony. This building bears many evidences of having been the residence of one of the Doges, and there is one apartment that is especially worth inspecting—the suite to which it belongs being usually occupied by royalty when it passes this way. The walls and ceilings are richly decorated, and there are several emblems—notably the "Cap of Liberty" that gives good evidence of its having been occupied by one of the heads of the republic. The casings of the doors are of variegated marble, and the massive beams of the ceiling show the room to have been built a long time ago, and that it was intended to stand through many ages—a fact which has been fully verified.

But I must leave off writing and get ready to embark in the P. & O. steamer, which sails at 3 P. M. for Alexandria, Egypt. As we touch at Brindisi, Italy, I will close this at that place.

P. and O. S.S. " Assam," Brindisi, Italy, Sunday, Dec. 6, 1885.—We reached here yesterday morning, after a run of about thirty-four hours, the balance of the time being consumed in taking on cargo at Ancona and in waiting for daylight by which to enter the harbor. I've rarely ever seen a more quiet sea than we have had since leaving Venice, and the sky is beautifully bright. I hope it may continue so 'till we reach Egypt. We get quite an accession to our cabin passengers by the India mail train that left London on Friday night, and which reaches here at 1 A. M. to-morrow, and by daylight we shall be steaming toward the Land of the Pharaohs. At Alexandria we leave this ship and proceed by rail to Suez, where we meet the Nepaul, which takes us to Bombay.

V.

VENICE TO THE RED SEA.

P. & O. S.S. "ASSAM,"
AT SEA, NEARING ALEXANDRIA,
December 8th, 1885.

I CLOSED my last at Brindisi, Italy, but had not told you anything of the character of the various ports we touched at ; hence it is not unseasonable to retrace our steps and go back to Venice, the starting point on this journey to the East. The entrance to the harbor of this city is made through a narrow and tortuous channel, the line of which is well defined by a series of wooden piles, in some cases driven in clusters—some of these sufficiently strong to bear a heavy strain, as at the narrow turns the ship had to be warped around.

The distance from Venice to the Adriatic, I should judge to be from four to five miles, which took us about one and one-half hours to run. The depth of water in the channel is about 24 feet, but the harbor about the city has a greater depth. I was told the rise and fall of the tide is about one foot. The approaches to the city appear well protected by military works, and every available spot through the marshy district, which lies below the town, is fortified. At Ancona, which we reached in twelve hours from Venice, we found a very snug and much deeper harbor, and vessels of the largest class can lay quite close to the town. This small harbor is almost entirely artificial, and is protected from the heavier storms by the form of the coast, aided by artificial breakwaters of stone. The town presented a pretty appearance from the ship, and a number of our passengers consumed the time passed there—some four hours—in strolling through it and visiting an old cathedral prominently located on the heights.

Brindisi, some 400 miles from Venice, has quite a spacious harbor, which is well protected, both naturally and artificially. A prominent island, with a picturesque fort upon it, is immediately opposite the entrance, and there is ample room after crossing the bar for a large fleet ; but the depth of water does not permit the entrance of a large class of vessels. The present depth, both here and at Venice, is kept up mainly through dredging.

Now let us turn our attention to the good ship "Assam" one of the numerous fleet—51 in all—run by the " P. and O." Company. One of the most interesting features about her is the crew and cabin

boys, as they bring me, for the first time, in contact with the people of the East.   The working sailors are called Lascars, and come from the west
coast of India, about Surat, and are Musselmen in
religion.   They are lightly-built men not possessed
of any great physical strength, but many have intelligent and regular features, especially those selected
for petty officers.   All have dark complexion and
straight black hair, and among themselves speak Hin-
dostani but know sufficient English to understand
the commands of their officers.   The firemen and
coal-heavers are chiefly Africans, and most of them
come direct from that country.   The usual characteristics of that people are prominent; short, curly
hair, thick lips and broad, flat noses prevailing.   The
under-stewards and cabin boys are Portugese
Indians—that is, descendants of those who were first
taught the Christian religion by the Portugese, who
were the first European settlers at and about Bombay.   They are bright, intelligent fellows, who speak
more or less English and are most respectful.
" Picto " looks after my cabin and " Sanches " waits
upon me at the table.   All the above classes have
over them a certain number of English officers—engineers and stewards—who have the direct management of the various departments.   The ship is roomy,
and is provided with large, square ports, adapted for
a tropical climate.   Most of the cabins are arranged
for three persons, but they rarely fill them.

The India and Australia mail, which we received on board at Brindisi, is a large one, numbering over 900 sacks. No doubt the Xmas holidays have done much towards swelling it to this great bulk by home contributions of books and Xmas cards to their friends resident in India; but I learn that the natives are large subscribers to English journals and periodicals, and an examination of the post office book for India tells me, there are 8,000 post offices in the Empire, widely distributed. Truly, the English Government, in its paternal character, gives the native some return for taxes imposed.

The police and discipline, under Captain Cole, are excellent, but these ships have not all the conveniences found in the passenger vessels of the Atlantic trade. Their speed, too, is but something more than twelve miles per hour. Under this speed, and by the schedule, we reach Alexandria, 825 miles from Brindisi, on December 10, and leave the same morning (by rail), and arrive at Suez, 220 miles from Alexandria, that evening. We start at midnight on Thursday and reach Aden (1,308 miles) on the 15th, remain six hours, to " coal up," and then arrive at Bombay, 1,664 miles from Aden, on Tuesday noon (22d inst). Whole distance from Venice by this route, 4,400 miles. It is a little longer *via* Port Said and the Canal.

Hotel Suez, Suez, Egypt, December 11, 1885.—We had a detention of 12 hours at Alexandria, which was not disappointing, as it made a pleasant break in the journey and enabled us to have a comfortable drive in and about the city. A party of us passed a part of the morning in driving through the principal streets and visiting the various bazars. We also visited the forts, which still show the destructive effects of the English bombardment. That portion of the city about the " Grand Square," and which was burned during the siege, is being rebuilt in a superior style to that which obtained in 1875, when I was last in Alexandria. In the course of this drive we passed the Mahamoud Canal, and several gardens bordering upon it, rich in tropical plants and flowers. I saw numerous flowers of the *poinsettsia*, the leaves of which were as large as my hand, and *oleanders* that were in full bloom and almost as large as trees. There were also numerous *cacti*, and the fragrance from the sweet-scented *acacia* was delicious. *Morning glories*, in full bloom, were climbing nearly every protected wall—quite a contrast, is it not, to the character of vegetation and temperature that this will find you in ?

The older parts of Alexandria are very picturesque indeed ; the projecting or over-hanging stories of the houses ; the Moorish blinds to the windows ; the bazars with the workmen sitting in front of their doors—all engaged in manufacturing various articles, particularly in silver and gold ; the narrow streets ; picturesque Moorish costumes, and the varied scene one meets with will all tend towards making it, especially to the new-comer, a novel and interesting sight, that is in pleasing contrast to the land one has just left ; but the smells encountered do not incline one to linger long in the quarters especially occupied by the Arab.

The afternoon I passed with Commander Nicoll Ludlow, U. S. Navy, a Suffolk County man, who commands the snug little steamer Quinnebaug, then lying in the harbor, and which he keeps in tip-top order. I was invited to inspect his vessel, and every part of her showed the closest attention to police and discipline. The men looked contented and remarkably healthy. He had not a man in hospital out of two hundred. He greeted me with genuine Long Island hospitality, and in his steam launch we made a tour of the Harbor of Alexandria, where he pointed out the various objects of interest. We also visited the Khedive's yacht—a very spacious and richly decorated vessel, and after giving me a very comfortable and homelike dinner, he bid me good speed on my voyage, as the train was starting for this place. As the run was made by night, we saw but little of the canal, but from daylight 'till 7 A. M. we passed near enough to see numerous large steamers ploughing their way, as it were, through the desert.

As we reach here in advance of the Nepaul—the steamer which is to take us through the Red Sea to

Bombay (she having been detained by rough weather on her voyage to London and by fog on the canal) —we have passed the day rather profitably by visiting the street and bazars of this old town (once the starting point for the overland mail by coaches to Alexandria), and also by a ride on donkeys to the offices of the Canal Company, which are pleasantly located near its mouth.   Here we were permitted to inspect the system by which the officers can see at a glance the location of any ship that has entered the canal from either mouth.   I also saw some figures that give one a good idea of its enormous traffic. While in 1870 the number of vessels was only 486, of 436,609 tons—dues about $870,000—in 1884 the number of vessels was 3,284; tonnage 5,871,500; and dues amounting in round figures to over $11,-700,000.

We go on board the Nepaul about sunset and by 1 o'clock will be steaming down the Red Sea.

P. and O. Stmr. Nepaul, Red Sea, (Lat. 15° N.), Dec. 15th, 1885.—We sailed promptly at the hour above named, and have been making good time towards Aden, where I shall mail this. The Red Sea has proved a very quiet one to us, but hot, as I believe it always is. The prevailing breeze is from the north —hence we have had it following us—but as every convenience is made to provide against heat we have not suffered. It is only in the cabins and on the sunny side that one experiences any discomfort. On

deck, with a double awning, it is almost always pleasant, but I am told that in the summer time the heat
is intense.   I think the highest the thermometer has
marked has been 87 degrees. Passengers are allowed to take their mattresses on deck, which gives
one comfortable nights and refreshing sleep.   The
"punka," or table fan, was started the second day
after leaving Suez, so that all our meals are taken
with a gentle current of wind blowing over the table.
There are some features of this sea that are striking
and deserve notice—not the least attraction being
the superb sunsets which we had while in the Gulf
of Suez—the upper portion of the sea.   The coloring,
combined with the highly-marked outline of the
mountains which have a reddish tint, produced an
effect at sunset that I've rarely seen surpassed—and
the red coloring of its rocky shores would seem to
have given it the name of Red Sea.   At least it's
the best explanation I can learn, for there is certainly nothing peculiar about its waters.   The rise and
fall of the tide at Suez, is often eight or nine feet, and
is felt some miles up the canal.

I meet on board this ship a large number of India-
bound passengers, the major part being made up of
military and civilian officials returning to their posts.
All have been exceedingly kind and polite, and I've
learned many details of the inner life of the Indian
native.   We have on board Surgeon Hewlett, whose
duties are confined to inspecting certain districts, re-

porting upon their sanitary conditions and recommending the best modes of improving them. There is also an Inspector of Prisons, who is full of information and has given me many interesting facts. The Collectors, of which there are several on board, are very entertaining men. Their duties, in addition to collecting the Government revenue, are somewhat magisterial, and in the tours through their districts— often embracing areas of country twenty-five by fifty miles in extent, and containing 7,000,000 of people— they exercise the duties of magistrates, settling disputes between farmers, etc. The roads are also largely in their charge. They are thrown more intimately in contact with the people than almost any other class, and are often for weeks camped in their midst. The details of the domestic life and of the household, the hours of labor, of repose, and of their meals, as also their ceremonies, are all familiar to these officials, and they have suggested that I pass a few days with a Collector while on his round, which I may do if time permits.

We reach Aden to-morrow about noon, and will probably pass a few hours and add some coal to our present stock. I'm informed that the chief objects of interest are "The Tanks," constructed in Roman times for the storage of water. They are in the hands of the English, and rightly, too, for no nation is so deeply interested in keeping this route to the East open for traffic. My Xmas dinner I expect to eat in

Bombay, and as evidence of Indian hospitality, I will add, that I've already been asked to dine on that day by Mr. and Mrs. W——r, two as agreeable and interesting people as we have on board, and long residents of Bombay.

VI

ADEN TO BOMBAY.

P. AND O. STMR. "NEPAUL," INDIAN OCEAN.
(LAT. 17° N., LONG. 63° E., "LINE OF NO VARIATION.")
Sunday, December 20th, 1885.

IT is not often that a Long Island man crosses the line of "no variation," in the Indian Ocean—hence I gave it a prominent place in the heading of this letter. It is probably superfluous to tell your readers that this line is where the magnetic meridian and the true meridian coincide—or, in other words, that the needle of the compass points to the true north and there is no variation either to the right or left, as is usually the case.

We were a day late in reaching Aden, but that did not prevent our making the usual stop of six hours—time sufficient to see everything of interest. We were on shore by 2 P. M. of the 16th—landing at the post office pier. After securing the necessary stamps and mailing our letters, we hired a covered carriage, drawn by a small, but active pony, for an excursion to the old town of Aden and " The Tanks " near it. The charge was not high—being less than 50 cents for a drive of five miles and back. As we passed along the shores of the harbor we saw numerous large coal yards belonging to the various steamship companies trading to the East, all of which gave evidence of the importance of this place as a coaling port on the route to and from the Isthmus of Suez ; and here I wish to add that England has shown her foresight in the acquisition and holding of such strategic coaling points as Gibraltar, Malta, the Island of Perim, Colombo and Singapore, Hong Kong and Shanghai, etc.—places so essential to a commercial nation like her, whose vast commerce penetrates to the extreme East and to the furthermost points in the Southern Hemisphere—and I, for one, am heartily glad that she does hold them, as good government, free and fair trade, excellent police, broad and well-kept streets and good public conveyances usually attend where she controls.

In reference to the occupation of Perim—an island in the narrowest part of the Straits of Babelmandeb, and about ninety miles from Aden—I must relate the story, as given by a fellow-passenger, a Judge from India. It appears that, many years since, the French had fitted out an expedition for its occupation, which stopped at Aden *en route*. While being entertained by the English commander it leaked out whither the party was bound. The Aden commander at once secretly despatched a party to occupy it, so that when the French arrived they found the English flag flying, and were necessarily defeated in their purpose.

We found the old city of Aden, which lies in the crater of an extinct volcano, built in the Moorish style, with wide streets and a central square, around which are numerous cafés, where the natives were enjoying themselves in various ways. "The Tanks," which are at the farther end of the old town, date back to an earlier period, and show evidence of good engineering skill. They are capable of holding 8,000,000 gallons, which would be a most useful supply in case of siege. I believe most of the water now consumed is from distillation of sea water—the tank water is being reserved for an emergency. Aden is far from attractive-looking, and I fancied it would be shunned by the military, but was assured by an officer who had been stationed there that he did not regard it, by any means, as the worst of English military stations.

In the course of our drive we met numerous trains of camels packed with various articles of merchandise, which they were conveying to the interior. These packs weigh about 300 pounds each. The animals follow in single file and move at the rate of about three miles an hour—their Arab drivers following on foot or riding other camels. Among them were some fine specimens of men—tall, erect, and rather handsome-featured fellows, who stepped out with a vim. Still, neither their legs nor arms showed much muscular development, and I fancy they are little given to hard work. Every care seemed to be given to the protection of the head from the burning sun, and immense turbans of varied colors covered them, but their bodies were often attired with only the scantiest description of clothing. We met one or two patriarchal-looking men wearing the green turban—an unmistakable sign, I was told, that they had made the pilgrimage to Mecca—and they looked so well satisfied that I'm sure they were enjoying the fruits of the long journey to their Holy Land.

The harbor of Aden owes its protection to the formation of the coast, and the port lies at the upper end of quite an extended bay. It is here the Governor resides and the various steam lines have their agencies. The old town is five miles away, but is connected with the port by an excellent Mcadamized road. I judged from the appearance of the shores that there was a very considerable tide, and upon inquiry found that its rise and fall were between eight and nine feet.

I will finish this letter on reaching Bombay (where we expect to be on the 22d), merely adding that our voyage has been an exceedingly pleasant one, with very fine weather—the slight breeze which we've enjoyed being ahead and serving to cool the ship. The temperature has risen from 75 degrees to 80 degrees Farenheit. and, that you may the better appreciate the calmness of the sea, I will say that since leaving Suez there has been dancing on deck nearly every evening.

Byculla Club, Bombay, Friday, Xmas, 1885.—It is 81 degrees in the shade, and I've wandered about this immense establishment hoping to find some cool spot in which to complete this letter, begun on the 20th inst., and have finally settled upon the "Hon. Secretary's" desk in the basement, where I find the faintest possible breeze; and here on a Xmas morning, I purpose giving some impressions of Bombay, for first impressions are apt to be most vivid and most heartfelt.

We entered the harbor and cast anchor at 5 P. M. on the 22d. Our good ship, having been pushed a little, responded and brought us in on schedule time. Our anchorage was immediately opposite the fort, as it is still called, although at the present time there is no evidence of any military work, and the Government has appropriated it as sites for its various public buildings—many of them being superb structures and nearly all built in a semi-Moorish style—combining the best features of the Gothic with those of the Oriental. As we steamed in, Malabar and Colaba Points showed up well and we could detect, by the aid of our glasses, the handsome residences of the Europeans and rich natives, which cover the former, embowered in a mass of tropical vegetation. Prominent among the residences is Government House, the winter residence of the Military Governor. In the far distance the Ghauts Mountains were discernible, whose clay looking sides, enveloped in a slight haze, gave to them a peculiar effect. An immense fleet of merchant vessels of nearly every nationality lay at anchor near us, and the harbor seemed spacious enough to contain a good share of the shipping of the world. Altogether it is one of the most extensive and picturesque harbors I've ever visited.

The Port Surgeon had hardly boarded us before we were surrounded by as motley and varied crafts as one often meets with—from the snug steam launch to the native boat, with its graceful lateen sail and picturesque sailors; conspicuous among which were the Parsees, whose striking black hats at once attract your attention. I could liken it to nothing better than a section of a stovepipe with its upper part cut off at an angle less than forty-five degrees, and with its base set into a sort of cup to fit the head. The Parsee priests wear the same shaped hat, but of white material. We soon passed the inspection of the Customs official, were warmly greeted by some European friends, who were on the lookout for us, and sailed to the landing place at the Apollo Bunder, and, climbing a long flight of stone steps (for the rise and fall of the tide is from 18 to 19 feet), were in India.

A drive of two and a half miles, through the dusty, populous streets of the old town, brought us to this spacious and comfortable club, where I am most comfortably placed—for all of which I feel grateful to my kind friend, Mr. Pickering Clark, one of Bombay's most useful citizens, and to whom that city largely owes her well-conducted and excellent tramway system. I've thoroughly inspected its stables, shops, and offices, and for good order, thorough construction, and neatness of appearance they compare well with similar systems in any section of the globe. Mr. Clark is ably seconded in his work by Mr. George A. Kittredge, another American gentleman and a twenty-five years' resident of Bombay.

To give you an idea of the care bestowed by this company upon its horses, I can add that when the sun has great power, not an animal is hitched in—, without having a light cork hood, attached to the head stall and raised above the animal's head: The result is that they are rarely overcome by heat and sunstroke, and while 1 am told the loss of animals from over-fatigue and other causes, and on street railroads, in New York City, is about 10 per cent, here it does not exceed 7.

As I'm making this letter rather lengthy, I must reserve for another, some descriptions of the street scenes and the varied objects of interest to be met with here. Before closing, however, I must introduce to you "Ramah," the gentle Hindoo servant, who is to be my attendant in this trip through a part of India. Fancy to yourself a man of about thirty years; of medium height and light build; rather regular features; color something darker than mulatto: and clothed in a species of white tunic extending to the knees (called angurker), and with white pants; to this add a gorgeous turban of red and gold, with blue sash about the waist, and you have a rough pen picture of the native who is to serve me (unless he proves unfaithful) till I depart for more Eastern lands. He has been, now, two days in my service, and you can imagine how oddly it seemed when, last evening, upon entering the dining room of Mr. and Mrs. C. A. Winter, who had kindly asked me to dine with them, to find "Ramah" at the back of my chair; but, like all things else, one soon accomodates himself to new customs. At some houses I would not have had any attention unless provided with a servant of my own; the only exception to this is Government House, where one is not expected to bring their own servant, but at all other houses, dinners or evening entertainments, you take your own attendant. This applies equally to all railway stations and hotels. I pay what is regarded as rather a high price for "Ramah's" services $10 per month, but he finds himself with board and lodging; of course I pay his railway fare, which third class is about one cent per mile.

VII.

HINDOO AND PARSEE.

BYCULLA CLUB, BOMBAY.
(LAT. 18 53´ N., LONG. 72 53´ E., TEMP. AT 8 A. M., 75°)
December 30th, 1885.

I HAVE been more than a week in Bombay, and it's not unreasonable that you ask for my impressions.—"Is it disappointing, or are you pleased, and what are some of its striking features?" So far 'from being disappointed. I'm not only pleased, but it has even surpassed my expectations ; and, excepting Cairo, in Egypt, I know no city that furnishes so great a variety and is so decidedly Eastern in its details, as well as in its general appearance, as this. Its location is superb—being upon a peninsula with a grand bay on one side and the Indian Ocean on the other—far the greater part of the city being on high ground, with its principal residences scattered over the hills and along the sea-shore, and it presents to me a most picturesque appearance. The views from Malabar Hill (one of its highest points) at sun-set, are among the most striking and beautiful I've ever seen.   It is in this vicinity that the rich Parsees and Hindoos have built their finest bungalows—some of them rivalling in extent, beauty of design and or-namentation the handsomest villas I've ever met with in any portion of the world.   Spacious grounds surround each, and scattered through them are rich tropical plants and trees, whose ample branches keep out a portion of the burning sun and give a most luxurious, as well as comfortable, appearance to these Eastern homes.   Many of them are temporarily oc-cupied by the European residents.

But it is the street scenes that are most diverting and interesting to me, and these are to be found mainly in the old town and in the populous districts, where in some instances 70 or 80 people occupy a single house.   Here, sitting in front of their little workshops or grocery stores, and in the street ped-dling their various wares, are to be found, at the cooler hours, the most varied collection imaginable, and these furnish the most interesting objects of study. The Hindoo, with his white dress and varied-colored turban ; the Mussulman, similarly clad ; and the rather neat and natty Parsee, are all to be found collected in these localities.   Only the lower classes of women are to be met in the streets—that is, ex-posed to the public gaze—excepting the families of the Parsees, who are no longer polygamists and seem anxious to follow the manners and customs of the English, with whom they've long been on the best of terms. The Parsee, when driven from his Persian home, sought the shores of the Indian Ocean above Bombay, and, showing skill in various descriptions of trade, he naturally attracted the attention of the earliest English settlers of this country, and as he has never, like the Hindoo, been the advocate of excessively youthful marriages, he has preserved his stature and vigor, which is shown both in his person and features.

In religion the Parsees are fireworshippers, but they endeavor, also, to preserve the purity of all the elements—hence the bodies of their dead are never committed to the ground, but are exposed in towers of high eminences, where they are devoured by vultures. The following description of the manner in which the dead are treated was given me by one of my fellow-voyagers : " It seems that in every Parsee house there is, near the stairway or well of the house, covered with lattice, an aperture. As soon as life has left the body of the deceased it is taken to this opening and lowered to the ground floor, where it is received by a class of priests called "Nesersala," or death men (as their presence in the house would pollute it, the body is lowered to them), who prepare it for the last ceremonies. After it is appropriately dressed in white, the forehead is smeared with a kind of butter called *ghie*, and immediately afterward the dog, which is always found in every Parsee house, is admitted. Should he go to the body and lick the forehead it is regarded as a good omen and evidence that the departed is enjoying Paradise ; but on the other hand, should he refuse, the decree has been purgatory. A procession is then formed of the friends of the deceased, preceded by the priests, who convey the body on a bier to the "Towers of Silence." Only the male relatives attend, and they are clothed in white and follow the corpse in pairs, each pair holding a white handkerchief between them. Having arrived at the main gate of the enclosure, the body is taken in charge of by another set of priests who carry the body to the tower intended for its reception. These towers, five in number, differ somewhat in size—the largest being about 270 feet in circumference and some 40 feet in height. The interior of each tower, which is open to the sky, is covered at a height of ten feet from the ground. with a circular-flooring, which slopes towards a central well and contains numerous open grooves on which the bodies are laid. The outer ring of this flooring, or one nearest the inner wall of the tower, is appropriated for men, and signifies good actions ; the second ring, signifying good words, is for women, and the inner ring, meaning good thoughts, for children. Before the body is taken into the tower— which is through an aperture in its wall a few feet from the gronnd—it is stripped of its clothing, which is cast into another tower. As soon as the priests retire, a cloud of vultures alight and in a few moments strip the bones of the flesh. A few days later the priests return and with long-handled pincers seize the bones and throw them down the central well, which is 40 feet or more in width, where they remain to be decomposed by air and rain. The moisture runs off into the ground through filters of charcoal and sand, and leaves only the bones to crumble into their natural elements. I visited these towers one evening near sunset, and found the grounds about them converted into a beautiful garden. There were numerous vultures sitting on the tower edge and perched upon the trees about. Every portion of the grounds was scrupulously clean and neat. I was told that the priests who perform these various services in connection with the dead are a distinct class, and do not mingle with the other members of the Parsee community. They live apart from the world, and often in small colonies made up entirely of their own sect, and their marriages limited to members of their own calling—in truth, while regarded as necessary, they are shunned by their fellow Parsees.

The guide, who accompanied me, showed everything but the interior of the towers; but there was a working model of one, which he fully explained, and I then, after giving him a few "annas" (three cents each), withdrew to a prominent point on the hill to view the harbor and city and witness a most glorious sunset, for the views from the hill where the towers are located are the best in the city. Coming down, I got into my carriage and drove along the sea shore and, it so chanced, passed the cremating enclosure of the Hindoos. Thinking I'd make a single day of this species of sight-seeing, I descended, and entering the main gate was conducted by a rear passage to a point where I could witness the burning without being seen by the mourners. The corpse is placed between dry and inflammable logs of wood, which are confined in iron ricks, and I believe the torch is applied by some friend of the deceased. I saw some mourners sitting near, beating drums and uttering lamentations; but not fancying either the sight or odor, I did not tarry long; but I was told that all that remained after cremation was gathered up and cast into the sea, as in like manner is done along the shores of the sacred rivers Jumma and Ganges.

Among the most interesting places that I have visited in the city have been the stables of Arab and Persian horses. My friend, Mr. Clark, is an admirable judge and proved an excellent guide, as he is well known by the proprietors of the best stables. Those of Abdool Rayman are but a short walk from the Club, and contain some of the best Arabians in India. He has "Young Revenge," a beautiful bay, who has won more races than any horse in India. "The Doctor," a handsome white in an adjoining box stall, has sometimes beaten him. There were about three hundred horses in these stables, and among them were some fifty Persians—an animal not as much esteemed as the Arab. Another morning we visited the stables of Abdul Rizak Dobachell, who had also a fine stud—I believe about four hundred Arabs and Persians. He is regarded as a fair dealer, and his stables are popular. All these animals—as, in fact, everywhere in India—are hobbled with long ropes about their hind hocks, and these ropes are tied to a peg some feet in the rear. Their halters, or head-stalls, are also attached by cords to pegs on each side of them, and the animal takes his hay directly from the ground or floor of the stall. The system applies as well to the cavalry service, thus dispensing with the picket rope, which we use in the United States Army. I notice, with animals not stabled and much exposed to the sun, the headstall is provided with a fringe which falls over the eyes for their protection. Not the least striking feature of these stable scenes is the group of Arab horse dealers that one usually finds sitting just within the entrance of the stables. We were invited to take a cup of coffee with them, which I found excellent—being made from the true Mocha. They are tall, fine-looking men, with rather Roman features—prominent noses—and their costumes of rather rich colors are picturesque ones. They usually have two or three Persian or Angora cats with them, which they bring from their homes and which command good prices. Puss is usually tied, by a cord about her neck, to a post and seems to be used to it. These men also bring over some flat-tailed sheep, which one finds roaming about the stables.

While upon the subject of animals I must not forget the Hindoo bullocks, which are used by the natives before their odd-looking vehicles. These are small compact animals of about ten hands in height, and move with great quickness—some of them making as good time as the ponies of the country. I'd like to describe, also, the carriage that a pair of these fellows pull, but it's rather beyond my descriptive powers. Nor can I think of anything on Long Island or elsewhere in the United States that I might liken it to. I can simply state that it is a two-wheeled affair on springs, with two seats, and has a round-shaped body, highly ornamented in flaming colors, with a top and white curtains to protect the occupants from the sun. The driver sits astride the tongue and urges the bullocks forward by a kick or poke of his foot in the rear and a twist of the tail. A pair of rope reins passes over the head and through the noses of the animals, and with these he guides them. I've not taken a ride in this style of vehicle, but intend to, for I've taken a great liking to these bullocks, and wish to ride behind them. I'm sure your readers would have been amused if they could have been on the road with me this afternoon

and seen a grocery wagon, not unlike one of Park &
Tilford's very finest, drawn by a pair of these animals; only in this instance the wagon was marked
"Kemp & Co., Limited," and the bullocks were
creamy white, large-sized animals.

I'd like to tell you more of this amusing city, but
I can't spare the time, as I must make preparations
for continuing my journey toward the North.
Through the kindness of Colonel Upperton, of the
Bengal staff, I have been asked to take a seat in the
special train which leaves for Delhi to-morrow
night, and before going I've lots to do, including a
dinner I give this evening, at this club, to a few
friends, and one I attend at the Yacht Club, given by
Col. Rivett Carnac to-morrow night, when we dance
the old year out and the new year in. I shall there
meet a large number of Bombay residents. Were it
not for the heat of this place, I should be sorry
to leave, as I found it most entertaining and have
experienced nothing but hospitality from the moment of entering the city.

"Ramah" and myself continue to get on well together, and I feel satisfied I shall find him a useful servant in my wanderings about India. I observed that
he has added to the number of silver rings that he
first wore, so I imagine he has invested a share of the
advance made him in these adornments. I rather
think however, he has his mind upon some from Delhi
which is rather famous for its gold and silver works.

VIII.

THE CAMP OF EXERCISE.

BYCULLA CLUB,
BOMBAY, INDIA.
Tuesday, December, 30, 1885.

I PROMISED you a few items, from some point in my journey to the East, and this may do as well as any other for a commencement, especially as I can announce the arrival of the officers invited to attend the grand manœuvres of the Indian Army, or, as it is more frequently called, "The Camp of Exercise;" a term which appears particularly applicable, for, since the 15th of December, the two forces have been assembling about Umballa and Delhi, the former called the Northern and the latter the Southern Force. A course of drill and instruction has been going on ever since—first, under their brigade commanders; second, under their divisional chiefs ; and now they are manœuvring separately, but after the 2d of January the two forces are to engage in mimic warfare, gradually approaching each other, and during the last ten days of the exercise fighting over old historic ground, where *Ackbar*, the Great Mogul, gained his decisive victories, and where the mutiny of 1857 was stamped out. But to return; the officers, alluded to above, came in on the Peninsular and Oriental steamer *Assam*, on Monday, and are all in excellent spirits. They were at once taken to Watson's Hotel, the finest in the city, and were each assigned a servant, who will continue with them till the close of their military visit; some have Portuguese and others ye gentle Hindoo, but all speak sufficient English to enable them to come and go and satisfy the wants of those they are attending. Colonel Lazelle and Captain Mills of our Service by dint of close appilcation to travel, managed to reach Suez in time to join those from Europe, many of whom, coming on in advance, had taken in Cairo in Egypt. From Suez all have been under the care and kind protection of Colonel J. Upperton, C. B., of the Bengal Staff Corps, who is a charming man and a most excellent fellow, conversing with the various nationalities, he is thrown with, as glibly as possible. At this point he is joined by Captain A. L. Montanaro, also of Bengal Staff and likewise an excellent linguist, who seems to delight in doing kind and agreeable things.

There has been a round of dinners and lunches (tiffin) provided for the military guests, so that I imagine few have tested the Watson Hotel fare. The

first night they dined at the Yacht Club, a capitally
built and well managed-institution, located directly
on the harbor; a very pleasant feature of it is that
ladies are admitted, so that one lunches or dines in
their charming company; it also serves as a capital
point to meet their husbands and friends and take
tea after the business hours of the day, and then
probably off for a drive, as it is only in the cool of
the early morning or near sun-set that such open-air
recreation is possible, for the thermometer has marked
80° to 90° much of the time I've been here—nearly
ten days. Mr. Farnham, U. S. Consul, entertained
our officers and a few friends last evening; to-night
Lieut.-General Sir R. Phayre, K. C. B., Commander-
in-Chief of the military force in the Bombay Presidency, gives all the accredited officers a dinner; and
to-morrow night His Excellency, Lord Reay, Governor of Bombay Presidency, entertains them;
immediately after which they take a special train of
sleeping carriages, and start at 1 A. M. for Delhi, stopping one day at Jeypore, some six hundred miles
from here, for rest and sight-seeing; as Jeypore is
regarded as one of the handsomest cities in India, and
noted for its superb and extensive parks and flower-
gardens. In addition to the dinners and tiffins there
have been excursions to various points, such as visiting the "Caves of Elephanta," "Towers of Silence,"
"Malabar Hill," and drives along the sea-shore and
"Esplanade." I've not heard that any "*Nautch* danc-

ing parties have been visited, and if they had I don't think I'd tell who were there.

All the important Powers of Europe are represented, in this collection of officers. France has two representatives, one I believe a Major of Artillery, the other a Colonel of Cavalry. Germany has a Major and a Captain; the former, on occasions of ceremony wears an immense number of decorations, but some one has intimated that they were bestowed, mainly, for attending grand manœuvres, in various parts of Europe, rather than for service on the field of battle. Austria is represented by a Colonel of the Hussars, a very agreeable gentleman, and a member of the well-known Esterhazy family.

Russia has two officers, one a Colonel and the other a Russian Prince, but I have not learned the military rank of the latter.

Italy has sent two officers and one of these, a Brigadier-General, is the senior in rank of the entire group, and upon him devolves much of the duty of replying to speeches of welcome and toasts at dinners, &c., a duty that he modestly performs and I believe in a very happy manner; while he speaks English with tolerable fluency his remarks are usually made in French. Those from our Service I've alluded to before, one a Captain of Artillery, and the other a Lieutenant Colonel of Infantry.

The India Government took charge of these officers from the time of their arrival at Suez, and will defray all their expenses, up to date of their leaving the country, including their return passage as far as Suez. Nearly all, I believe, are to leave India shortly after the close of the manœuvres, the only exception that I've heard of, being Colonel Esterhazy, who told me he expected to pass the summer in Kashmir and the following winter here in India.

I am glad that I am able to say that I've greatly enjoyed my ten days' stay in Bombay, having met with an unbounded hospitality, and have also had a share in the entertainments provided for the military visitors accredited from the various countries. Through the kindness of Colonel Upperton I join the special train provided, and will have agreeable and congenial companionship *en route*, as I've found all the guests most delightful men. At Delhi I am promised, by the Military Secretary of General Roberts, a tent,—probably the other fixtures,—so that there is a good prospect of my seeing the manœuvres under favorable circumstances, and you may hear from me again before leaving India.

Northbrook Hotel, Delhi, Jan. 8, 1886.—I enclose the military scheme relating to the manœuvres now in progress. * * * The entire force is now some distance from this, and the *accredited* officers (who have a flying camp) near it. They are to return in the course of the next five days, which time I purpose consuming in a hurried trip to Amritzer and Lahore ; after this I return to my tent, which is in the head-quarters camp.

I have not seen any thing of the main body of troops. * * * The few native organizations that I have met are a fine-looking class—that is, as natives go. The police of all the cities visited are recruited from the Punjab, have good physique, and carry themselves well ; they salute all Europeans, as do also most of the natives, which keeps one busy when in the streets.

Delhi has proved rich in mosques and places formerly occupied by their great moguls, but the greatest treat is still in store in the Audience Halls and the superb tomb of "*Taj Mahal*," at Agra, which I take in on my way southward.

The following is the military scheme for the government of the manœuvres :

" The Southern Army Corps, numbering about 16,000 men, is now encamped before Delhi. The 1st and 2d Divisions, which were encamped at Sultanpur and Gurgaon respectively, have been concentrated with the right resting on Badlika-Serai, facing north, awaiting orders to move forward on the 4th January for the final manœuvres, of which the following is the ' problem ' issued from Army Headquarters :

Two hostile forces, distant 100 miles, are set in movement towards each other with the object of delivering battle as soon as contact occurs.

Their movements are restricted to the following daily marches:

For cavalry and horse artillery . .	20 miles.
For infantry and field artillery . .	15 "

Collision and separation of the forces after battle.

Reinforcement of one side and retirement of the weaker force under pursuit.

On the 3d January a field force, strength as follows: 2 infantry divisions, 2 cavalry brigades, 10 batteries artillery, 3 companies sappers and miners (about 16,000 men)—is encamped along the line Thol-Shahabad, facing south, its base at Umballa. Orders are received to march for Delhi with the idea of raising the seige of that place, then in progress.

On the same date a field force, strength as follows: 2 infantry divisions, 2 cavalry brigades, 10 batteries artillery, 3 companies sappers and miners (about 16,000 men)—which is covering the siege of Delhi, is encamped along the line Bahadurgah, Badlika-Serai facing north, when information is received that a hostile army moving south has passed Umballa.

The commander of this force is directed to march northward and deliver battle as far from Delhi as may be possible.

Operations are limited to the east by the line of the river Jumna; no restriction is placed on movements westward.

Operations will be carried on daily from 9 A.M. to 3 P.M., when the halt will be sounded, and no further movement will take place till 9 o'clock the following morning, by which hour the troops will be in position on the ground occupied by them at 3 o'clock on the previous afternoon.

Outposts will be thrown out, as on service, after the halt has been sounded, and will not be withdrawn until the divisional commanders have satisfied themselves that their position has been made secure from sudden attack.

It is desirable that troops should be encamped or bivouacked as near as possible to the positions occupied by them at the close of each day's proceedings, having due regard to the position of the supply depôts.

Camps, hospitals, baggage, transport animals, are not liable to capture.

The time should be regulated daily by the Chief Umpire's watch.

Infantry will not be conveyed on gun-limbers, carts, or animals during the manœuvres.

These manœuvres will, no doubt, fully test the marching powers of both Army corps, as well as their organization and equipment.

* * * * * * *

The following remarks have been made by the Umpire-in-Chief (General Sir Frederick Roberts, Commander-in-Chief in India), on the operations of the 7th January, 1886.

* * * * * * *

" The lesson we have learned to-day is the inutility of bodies of mounted troops pushing on at an unusually rapid rate without some very distinct objective, such as the seizure of a bridge over an unfordable river, or the occupation of a pass, or some very important position which it might be capable of holding until reinforced by infantry.

"Under such circumstances it would be permissible on the part of a commander to force the pace even at the risk of losing a certain number of horses, but when no such objective is to be attained, or when the position is one which can be avoided, or turned by any enemy, such rapid movement is a waste of power.

"On the present occasion Brigadier-General Marter reached Paniput at an early hour yesterday, but was forced to retreat this afternoon by the cavalry of the Southern Force supported by its 1st Division of infantry.

"With reference to this day's proceedings the following points call for observation:

"*The Southern Force.*—Had the reconnaissance in force which Sir C. Gough originally intended to make on Paniput been carried out, the weakness of the enemy would probably have been ascertained, and a forward movement would have obliged Brigadier-General Marter to retire.

"For want of this information the commander of the Southern Force hesitated to attack until his infantry arrived, while his cavalry, consisting of two brigades with 12 guns, was kept in check by one brigade of the Northern Force with 6 guns, without the latter having any material advantage of ground. During the 3½ hours the Southern Cavalry remained stationary the main body was too close to its pickets, and was kept mounted unnecessarily; moreover, no adequate means were taken to guard the flanks.

"The action of the cavalry of the Southern Force was slow, and showed a want of dash and enterprise throughout the day's proceedings, more especially on the left; if this portion had been boldly used it would have seriously harassed the retreating enemy; as it was the Northern Cavalry were allowed to retire with little or no loss.

"No attempt apparently was made to scout in any direction either beyond the canal to the left or towards the Jumna to the right; scouts well pushed to either flank would have inevitably gained much valuable information and might possibly have enabled the Southern Cavalry to advance at an earlier hour, and to throw its entire strength upon the communications of the Northern Cavalry.

"Owing to a want of proper scouting, a half battery of E-A Royal Horse Artillery came into action within easy (700 yards) range of a well-posted body of dismounted cavalry.

"The march of the divisional artillery and infantry was well timed and the attack on Paniput well directed.

"With regard to the advance of the infantry, however, the special attention of commanders is drawn to the instructions contained in Adjutant-General's memorandum issued on 19th ultimo, which point out that during the early part of an advance, no more men should be brought into the fighting line than are actually required for fighting purposes. This order was not complied with in the formation of the infantry during the advance on Paniput, two companies (four half-companies) per battalion being extended before the troops came under any fire whatsoever. At that stage of the advance, only sufficient men to cover the front of each battalion should have been extended, the remainder of each company forming supports, which should have moved in such formation as the nature of the ground might admit of, the main object being to keep the maximum number of men as long as possible in hand in a close formation until the fire of the enemy compels the attacking line to be strengthened.

"The six batteries of field artillery which came into action on the arrival of the 1st Division, were apparently firing at an indefinite object, and subsequently were not moved forward in sufficient time to prepare the way for the infantry, whose advance they were supposed to be covering.

"*The Northern Force.*—The commander of the cavalry of the Northern Force carried out effectually the difficult task assigned to him. With one brigade of cavalry he held his ground and compelled the enemy to develop his attack with the whole of his cavalry, six batteries of field artillery, and one infantry division; his retirement was carried out in good order, aided by his second brigade which came up in time to support his right.

"On both flanks the scouting was good, and the action of small parties pushed forward to ascertain the whereabouts of the enemy was effective.

"Several parties of dismounted cavalry were well placed and did good work, notably one of the 14th Bengal Cavalry under Major Harenc.

"The guns of L-A Royal Horse Artillery were judiciously posted in three separate divisions, and by their fire materially checked the advance of the Southern Force.

"Three guns of F-A Royal Horse Artillery had to be put out of action on the right of the Northern Force, in consequence of being charged by a regiment of cavalry who came upon them at the moment their escort was dismounted and consequently unable to act.

"The camp of the cavalry commander of the Northern Force should have been struck and packed ready for loading, in case retirement took place.

"Paniput remains in possession of the Southern Force, but had the commander of the Northern Force been aware that he was at liberty to push his infantry in movement near enough to support his cavalry as the Southern commander did, to-day's operations might possibly have had a different result."

IX

BOMBAY TO DELHI.

NORTHBROOK HOTEL, DELHI,

LAT. 28 N.; LONG., 77 E., TEMP. 63°.

January 8th, 1886.

THE ride from Bombay to this place, which we reached on the 3d inst., proved a very pleasant one. We started, as was proposed in my last, from Calaba Station, in Bombay, at 1.30 A. M. on the first day of the year—after witnessing a very pretty dancing party at the Yacht Club, where some of the best people of the city had assembled; and after seeing the old year out and the new year in — singing, at the same time, "Auld Lang Syne,"—we bade good-bye to our guests and went to the station in time to get well stowed away previous to the hour of starting. Ample accommodations had been secured by Colonel Upperton, English Army, and each compartment was provided with the necessary refreshments for the journey. As each one had secured in advance a pillow, a comforter and a couple of wraps (all of which articles are absolutely necessary for travel in India), it mattered not whither we went. We had our beds made up on the long seats with which these railway carriages are provided. As the first 160 miles were made at night, I saw nothing of the country along the line—which was that of the Baroda, Bombay and Central India Railway—but I know from the map that the road runs near the coast, in a northerly direction, just far enough to head the numerous little indentations in it, and that we reached Surat at 8 A. M., where we had a most comfortable breakfast.

Shortly after leaving Surat we crossed the Tapti River, a very large stream. At this season the water is low and the river confined to a narrow channel, but the very wide, sandy, bed showed what a huge stream it could become in high water. It reminded me greatly of one of our Western streams. At Broach we crossed the Nerbudda, a river that rises far in the interior of India, and, I was told, would become in a few years a sacred one, like the Jumna and Ganges. The country along this section of the line indicated that it was cultivated at every point, and we passed numerous fields of millet, several large ones of the castor bean, and very extensive ones of winter wheat, now some five or six inches high, and which is gathered in April; it was sown in October and November. Some time in the after-noon we met with our first specimens of monkeys—

a long, ring-tailed species, which when running carry their tails in the air, curved almost into a complete circle. There were some groups of ten or fifteen. We also saw numerous birds, such as quail, a variety of the grouse, and doves and pigeons innumerable.

As this is the dry season, we had a good opportunity of observing the mode of irrigation, the water for which was drawn from wells either by the old well pole process—one man to each pole—or with bullocks, which pull the water up in immense skin buckets, the cord passing over a pulley, two sets of oxen being used. They build a ramp up to the edge of the well, down which the animals travel, thus giving them the full power of their weight and strength. As soon as the bucket reaches the top and is landed on the platform they are unhitched and travel around by another incline, and are ready for the next bucket. The water is poured into a trough and thus runs through the various irrigating ditches prepared for it, and thence into the little field—each household having about four acres of land on which to subsist, and of the product of this, I was told, one-third goes to the State. Rather heavy taxation, we would say; but I believe it has been the rate since the great mogul kings first conquered the country. The land is all owned by the Government, and the farmers lease from it, which leases are renewed from time to time.

We reached Ahmedabad at 4 P. M., where we

lunched. It is quite an important town, and has numerous mosques. It is also the headquarters of the Northern division of the Bombay Army. We arrived at Palanpore at 8 P. M., where we took our New Year's dinner, and after it continued our route, passing, about 11 P. M., near Mount Aboo, the highest elevation in our journey—some 2,000 feet. We reached Ajmar about 8 A. M., where we were taken in charge by some English officers and driven to their snug little club for breakfast, and after it inspected one of the summer palaces of the great Ackbar, chief of the Mogul kings, which is beautifully situated on the borders of an artificial lake. Sufficient of it remains to indicate the luxury which he enjoyed, and the rich decorations of the marble of which it is constructed tell that he employed the best talent of his day. From this we visited the palm gardens, but had not time to look through Mayo College, an institution for the education of sons of wealthy natives, whose minds are there given such a turn as will be for the interest of the State. It is now in charge of Major Loch of the English service, and he told me that the number of pupils was increasing and the institution flourishing.

Ajmar is beautifully situated, being in a pretty valley surrounded by an amphitheatre of mountains. I was greatly taken with its site and surroundings. As time pressed, we could not linger as long as we wished in this attractive spot, but were driven back to the station and resumed our journey—reaching Jeypoor about 1 P. M., where we lunched and at once took carriages in order to inspect that handsome town, which is one of the finest in India. It is a walled city, and, driving through its imposing gate, we came first to the School of Arts, where the youth are being instructed in drawing, modeling, etc. Their work showed considerable proficiency, and in the metal working department we purchased several of their constructions.

From this we drove to the palace of the Maharaja there, an inspection of which was very interesting, as it was my first introduction to the residences of these native princes. He is one of the richest of them, having an income of about £1,200,-000 ; £500,000 of this is required for the support of his Government, and the remainder he has for his own use and pleasure. Rather a handsome sum to live and sport upon. His palace, however, shows that he needs large funds, as it covers, with the grounds and gardens, an extensive area and can only be kept up with a large force. The first part of the palace we entered was painted in a dark pink, and in the centre of the court was the audience or reception room for the masses. Passing beyond this, we ascend by a gently-sloped ramp into the reception apartment for the higher classes of natives and where the great durbars are held. The throne upon which the Prince sits, during these audiences, is of

silver and gold, and the guide told us that the Europeans were seated on one side and the natives upon
the other. We also ascended the tower and had
some fine views from its summit. We could see the
apartments of his wives, but were not asked to
enter.

After descending from the tower, we inspected the
blue palace, which we reached by walking through a
handsome garden, where nearly every tropical plant
was being cultivated. In this were also very extensive arrangements for the display, on festive occasions,
of fountains and waterspouts. The entire area, I
should judge, covers about forty acres. We were
next shown the stables, which must contain some
fifty riding animals alone, and a share of carriage
horses of English breeds. The hostlers gave us
some exhibitions of their training, showing that the
Maharaja employs useful men. Leaving the stables,
we resumed our carriages and drove to Prince Albert
Hall, which contains some very interesting native
work—most of which is to be sent to an exhibition
to be held shortly in England. We also drove
through the gardens and saw the fine tigers, bears
and birds which form its zoological collection.

We were only "choked off" from further sight-
seeing by the coming of darkness, which, in the
tropics, follows almost immediately upon the setting
of the sun ; and driving to the Kaiser-I-Hind Hotel,
found an excellent dinner awaiting us, after which

THE JUMMA MUSJID, DELHI.

we returned to our train, which started at midnight for this city—reaching here the following morning (2d) at 10 A. M. We were driven at once to the headquarter-camp of General Sir Frederick Roberts, the Commander-in-Chief of the Indian Army, whom we found most genial and attractive. At the dinner given in the evening, where there were some forty ladies and gentlemen present, all made up from the military, he gave us a few remarks—chiefly to welcome the officers accredited from the various foreign Governments—which were exceedingly happy, and I can readily understand the warm attachment, I hear expressed on all sides, which both officers and men have for him.

As the seat of the great Mogul kings, I've found much in Delhi to interest me. They have left behind them many mosques and audience halls that are beautiful in design and rich in decoration. The Jam'i Masjid, or Great Mosque as it is more commonly known, is more imposing than any I've ever seen, those at Constantinople not excepted. It has superb gateways, and it's interior court (325 feet square), is capable of holding 10,000 men.

The external appearance of this superb mosque is very striking. It is built mainly of red sandstone and upon a slightly rocky eminence, and approached an three sides by grand flights of steps that lead up to its imposing gateways. The lowest of these steps is about 150 feet in length and they diminish as

they approach the top. Its gateways are 40 feet
high and surmounted by marble domes. The mosque
proper—or place of worship, has three large marble
domes. The minarets of the mosque rise to a height
of 130 feet, and contain stairways which enable one
to reach the top. I ascended one of these and had
a splendid view of the City of Delhi. It is said that
5,000 workmen were employed for six years in the
construction of this work. Near one of the gateways
are kept the sacred relics and writings. I was shown
a copy of the Koran written in *Kufik* about the VII.
Century of our era, a slipper of the Prophet filled with jasmine, footprint of the Prophet imprinted
on a stone, and a hair from the Prophet's mustache. A
venerable looking priest was the custodian, and his
appearance interested me.

The Diwan-I-Khas, or "Private Hall of Audience," where the King received his highest princes,
is a beautiful structure of white marble, ornamented
with gold and precious stones, and a nook where
one delights to linger. I've already passed some
hours in it and the Moti Masjid, or "Pearl Mosque,"
and always left them with regret. The latter is truly
a gem. It is built of exquisitely white marble, and
when you enter its court there is experienced a feeling of purity and repose I've rarely ever felt in any
other structure. You simply wish to sit down and
admire its beautiful proportions and examine its
chaste decorations, cut in relief, for there is no inlaid

work.   It appears to me that if I were a·resident of this city, nothing could give me greater pleasure than a daily visit, and it puzzles me how a people daily accustomed to see so much beauty and taste should not have risen above the level they now hold.

I have named what to me appear to be the gems of the city, but there are many other mosques and tombs scattered over the plains of Delhi—many ot them deserving close attention.   Eleven miles from this is the Kutoob Minar, a beautiful tower of 240 feet, built of a combination of light red and buff sand-stone and marble, that is greatly admired.   I'm not sure that I've ever seen a finer tower, and one can with pleasure examine its minutest details.   Murray, after describing it at great length, sums up by giving four particular points as constituting its chief attractions :   First, its great height;   second, the magnificent bands of inscriptions in Arabic that encircle it ;   the next point is its flutings and the fourth its perfect symmetry.   But I must bring this letter to a close as it is getting late and I start to-morrow on a hurried trip to Amritzer and Lahore, some 350 miles to the north of this—returning in time, I trust to witness the " March Past " on the 19th.

X.

DELHI TO LAHORE.

MONTGOMERY HOTEL, LAHORE, EAST INDIA,
(ABOUT LAT. 31° 30. N., LONG. 75° 45 E.
TEMP. AT 8 A. M., 55°.)
January 13th, 1886.

SINCE mailing my Delhi letter I've traveled to this city, some 350 miles further towards the northern frontier of India, and the limit of my journey in this direction. I could make the distance from this to Peshawur—300 miles beyond, and what may now be regarded as the extreme frontier station of India, in the northeast—very comfortably indeed ; but, as there is nothing in particular to be gained, and no ancient objects of interest to be met with, I shall turn back from this city—having in mind the fact that one who contemplates a journey around the world must consider what is before him, and not devote too much time to any particular country.

The city of Lahore is prettily situated near the river Ravee, and is an important one of the Punjab, distant from Bombay 1,238 miles, and in time 72 hours. As the junction of the Scinde, Punjab and

Delhi Railway, with the Indus Valley and Punjab Northern State Railway—the entire system is now known as the Northwestern Railway—its importance, both in a commercial and military sense, is very great. No doubt, in case of collision with Russia, this city would be important as a base of supplies.

But I must turn back a little and tell you of my trip from Delhi, which I left at noon on the 9th. We stopped some half hour at Ghaziabad (fifteen miles from Delhi) for lunch or tiffin—a term, by the by, more in general use in India than lunch. Ghaziabad is quite a railway centre, and here the line from Delhi joins the one from Calcutta, and on starting we found the number in our compartment increased by two—one of whom was Dr. Webb, an inspecting surgeon of the English service, who gave much valuable information concerning the country we were passing through.

The face of the country is very similar to that previously passed over, and is exceeding flat and level. A species of the mimosa, or acacia tree, scattered here and there, furnished the only variety. As you may imagine, fuel is expensive, and you naturally ask whence the native derives his supply. This is obtained from the " bois de vache," or droppings from cows and bullocks, which they mix with cut straw and make up into cakes, this they plaster on the side of their mud huts to dry, and I'm told it makes very good fuel. I've sometimes used the same on the frontier of our own country—where, as droppings from the buffalo, it is called buffalo chips, and have found it a very fair substitute for wood.

The country between Ghaziabad and Saharunpore, where we stopped, about 6 P. M., for dinner, is highly cultivated, and well supplied with water through artificial canals. The sugar cane is extensively grown, and I saw many fields of it still standing. As frosts are rare, I presume they can take their own time in gathering the crop. The stalk was small, and, compared with cane grown in Louisiana, very inferior. I saw no sugar works along the line, but was told that each planter had his own apparatus for crushing the cane and boiling the juice down to a proper consistency.

We awoke on the morning of the 10th at Umritzar, an interesting point on the line, and where we left the train. During the night we had passed Umballa, where travelers take stages for Simla—distant a day's drive. Those intending to go to Mossoorie another hill station and sanitarium, leave the line at Saharunpore. I had a very tempting offer from Mr. H. Vansittart, a barrister, to visit him at Mossoorie, and see a little of Indian hill life, but I resisted, knowing that I intended to make an excursion to Darjeeling, which is some 8,000 or 9,000 feet above the sea, and where I'd have an excellent opportunity of seeing the Himalaya Mountains.

Simla is the summer resort of the Viceroy of In-

GOLDEN TEMPLE AND LAKE, AMRITZER.

dia, and the chief officers of the Government are transferred to that point during the hot season. Most extensive and substantial public offices have been erected for their accommodation. Just fancy the Government at Washington transferred for the summer to St. Louis, Mo., and you can form an idea of the distance it is sent from the actual capital, Calcutta—something more than 1,200 miles.

Umritzar (or Amritzar), derives its name from the Sanskrit words (a,) (not,) (mrit,) (death,) (zar,) fountain signifying "fountain of immortality." The great attraction of the city is its golden temple. It is not a large structure, but beautifully situated in the midst of a lake of pure water. Built of marble, it has its upper portion covered with copper gilt, and the effect is very fine, particularly when the sun is shining upon it. As we approached the borders of the lake we were politely asked to take off our shoes and don a pair of slippers, which, of course, we did; and following the guide, we proceeded along the marble border of the lake, to a massive gateway, which guards the entrance, and is highly decorated. This gateway has on one of its side posts an inscription announcing that many years since (I forget the date) a thunderbolt passed through the temple without injuring the worshipers or doing any damage to the strcuure.

Passing through the gateway, we continued over a marble causeway to the temple itself, which is in the centre of the lake. Entering we found two or three jolly looking priests sitting behind the sacred writings of the Sikhs, which are contained in a large book called " The Granth." There were three others who were performing a weird kind of music on odd shaped instruments. Two had a species of violin, and the other, two drums upon which he beat the time with his fingers. A number of devotees were sitting about, saying their prayers and casting votive offerings on a sheet in the front of the priests, in return for which flowers, that been under the holy book, were given the worshipers. Some were given to me and I enclose you a few leaves. They will be withered by the time they reach Long Island ; still, they may have a charm. My servant, Ramah, being a good Hindoo went through all the necessary duties and was quite lavish with his copper coins, which he distributed among the priests and musicians. Many of the inlaid decorations of this temple (and most of the lower part of it is so finished) were brought by the Sikhs from the tomb of Iehangir, at Shahdera, near Lahore.

Amritzar is in the heart of the Sikh country, and they gave the English more trouble to subdue than almost any other tribe in the Punjab ; but, once subdued, they have been among the most loyal and devoted of her Majesty's subjects. They rendered excellent service to the British during the mutiny of 1857-8. They have fine forms, are stalwart and enterprising, and scarcely any finer specimens of the human race can be found anywhere. The secret of their success lies in their great endurance, rapidity of movement and the slight amount of food they carry when making long marches. I've omitted stating that we saw along the borders of the lake the sacred bull, a fine slick-looking specimen of the Hindoo animal. He was rubbing himself against the trunk of a tree at the time we were inspecting him, and seemed entirely satisfied with his position—but on no condition would they permit us to touch him.

There were other objects of interest about the lake, that attracted our attention. Some enterprising merchants were plying their trades, such as comb makers, sellers of steel ornaments, writers of Sikh books and Fakirs. The latter are religious enthusiasts, who devote their whole lives to what they deem religious service. They are not attractive looking men, with their half-naked bodies, long, matted hair, which is never combed, and their heads and faces smeared with ashes. Some distort their legs or arms by sitting in one position for a long period, or by holding the arm erect in the air until it becomes paralyzed. They often add to this by forcing the thumb nail into the palm of the hand. Still, they are received by even the higher classes, and you sometimes see them riding about in the carriages of the rich Marajahs.

The bazaars of the city contain large stores of

goods from various parts of the world, and here are manufactured some of the best articles to be found in the Punjab. Of course, I was a victim to these adroit traders who are about as persistent in their endeavors to dispose of their wares as any people I've ever met. A handsome rug, a pair of Pulgarees a large ivory cutter, and some other small articles were almost forced upon me, and although I beat them down to about one-third of the asking price, yet I imagine they made a good profit.

We found, in the course of an hour's drive about the suburbs of the city, that roses and various flowers grow well, as, also, the orange and lemon. Some of the orange groves that we passed were the largest I've yet met with. Handsome bungalows were located near, or in their midst, and I imagined their occupants had about as much comfort as anybody in India; for they have rather a temperate climate and are only compelled to resort to the hill stations during the very hottest months—viz., from July to October. For nearly four months fires are requisite, and the ruddy complexions of the Europeans we met gave evidence that they were not sufferers from the heat.

I visited the carpet and rug manufactory of one of their best firms, Davee, Sahai, Chumba, Hull, and saw a large number of looms in operation. All the articles here were hand-made, and they employed some three hundred or four hundred workmen, whom

they pay at a rate of from 15 to 35 cents per day —
depending upon the skill of the laborer. We would
regard such wages as excessively low, but when it
is remembered that their board and clothing cost
them but ten cents per day, it will be seen that they
are fairly well paid.

We completed our sight-seeing about 2 P. M., and
then drove to the railway station, where, by-the-by,
we had left our traps, as nearly all the large stations
in India are provided with cloak-rooms, where articles
can be left by paying six cents per package for each
day's care. We then ordered a comfortable lunch,
which was washed down with very good Scotch
whiskey and soda, usually styled a "peg," and at half
past three P. M. left for this city, which was reached in
two hours, and without meeting with any especial
object of interest.

From one of the minarets of a tomb at Amritzar,.
I had a fine view of the Himalaya Mountains, so that
one of the objects of my visit to India has been accomplished.

My time here has been so completely occupied by
sight-seeing that I've not had time to tell you of
this city, which is highly interesting in many particulars. Shortly after reaching it I was called upon by
the Rev. John Newton, of the American Christian
Mission, who gave me many interesting facts concerning the city and also some useful hints as to what
objects were most worth seeing, and further increased

my obligation by asking me to dine with him, which
I did, in company with Mrs. Newton and the Rev.
Mr. Formon and wife, of the same mission; so that I
had not only a comfortable, home-like dinner, but an
agreeable chat about home and home life. I was also
invited to inspect their school, which is large and
flourishing—native boys answering questions in English as promptly as one could wish. One little chap
of eleven, who gave me his name as "Surjon Dass,
Nation Sude, from Lahore," pointed out on a chart
my route to New York from this city and thence
around the world—I, of course, calling off the points
that I had passed and expected to pass in the course
of my journey.

Lahore is a very old city, and was noticed both by
Chinese and Greek travelers of an early date; but it
was not until some time in 1500 that the Moguls
made it a royal residence, and embelished it with
mosques, palaces and gardens. Its domestic architecture was also greatly improved, and there now
exists in the old portion of the city, some as fine
specimens and as picturesque house fronts as I've
met in India.

The oriole windows and carved window screens—
the latter so common in the East, and designed to
permit the wives of the owner of the house to see the
outside world without being seen themselves—are
especially noticeable. Some of the old mosques, now
greatly neglected, show rich coloring in various por-

tions, and although very old their freshness is thoroughly maintained.

Perhaps the greatest attraction to me was the old fort of Lahore, which contains the remains of a handsome palace, a very large mosque and a handsome mausoleum of Ranjit Singh—the latter a mixture of Hindoo and Mohammaden architecture ; but its effect is striking. In the centre, and immediately under the dome is a raised stone platform, on which are the marble urns which contain the ashes of himself, his four wives and seven concubines—the wives and concubines having been burned alive at the same time that his body underwent cremation. The urns are decorated with the lotus flower, save those of the concubines, which are perfectly plain. The urns containing the ashes of two pigeons that flew into the flame during the process of burning the bodies are placed on the border of the collection. Ranjit Singh was the last of the Mogul Kings. His son is now living in England on a handsome pension granted by the British Government, but I believe he is anxious to return, and I recently saw that his extensive landed property, with its well-stocked game preserves, was offered for sale. Perhaps he has been too extravagant.

It was in this city that the famous Koh-i-nur ("mountain of light") diamond was secured to the Queen of England. Tradition had it that this diamond came originally from the mines of Golconda, and as far

back as from 3,000 to 5,000 years B.C. It being
at first in the hands of the Hindoo rulers and afterwards possessed by the Musselmen. Baba, one of the
earlier of the Mogul conquerors, held it.   After that
it passed through various hands until it reached Shah
Sujah, who was treacherously imprisoned while on a
visit to Kashmir.   His wife visited Ranjit Singh, at
Lahore, and promised the diamond on condition of
his securing the release of her husband. His release
was finally effected, but not through the aid of
Ranjit.   He went by invitation to Lahore, where,
through persuasions of rather a harsh character—
such as having a guard placed about his person and
the reduction of an allowance of food—he yielded
it to Marahja Singh.   On the conquest of the Punjab it was, in 1849, given to the English and shortly
after presented to the Queen. What sort of persuasions were used to induce the holder to turn it
over to the English, history does not record. It has
been held at fabulous sums by the various possessors,
but I believe that its true value is about $1,000,000.

I have from Mr. David Ross in his book called " The land of the five rivers " that the wife of
Shah Sujah estimated its value in the following novel
manner. " According to what she had heard from
her ancestors, its value is equal to a heap of precious
stones and gold mohurs filling a space marked by
five stones, each thrown on four sides and upwards
by a strong young man. Some have declared even

this an inadequate estimate ; others have said that its value is equal to half the daily income of the · whole world. The real price at which it has passed from one hand to another is the submission of the weak to the powerful. That purchased it for the *Saduzai* family, and that transferred it at last into the hands of the Maharana.

As before stated, the fort at Lahore I found very interesting. The old palace within its walls indicates that the royal residence was a handsome one. I examined several of its apartments, and was struck with those formerly occupied as the living rooms, the ceilings being of various colored glass, as also the walls. The grand saloon, of glass and gold, must have been extremely rich in early days, and the effect at night, when lighted with numerous lamps, must have been brilliant.

Among the excursions, I made, was one to the tomb of Jehangir, some five miles from the city and on the opposite side of the Ravi River. The tomb with its enclosure still covers a large space, and both its internal and external decorations indicate that a large sum was expended in its construction. Many of the precious stones which were inlaid in the walls have been carried away, but there are still traces of great beauty. It was built by Nur Jehan ("Light of the World")—also called Nur Mahal—the favorite wife of the Emperor. In reaching it we crossed the river on a bridge of boats, the first I've met with.

The gardens of Lahore are both extensive and beautiful. Those named in honor of Lawrence show great care and have some rare plants. There is also a very respectable zoological collection attached to them. In the museum I found much to interest me. There are complete models of all the native vehicles and agricultural implements ; also correct representations of the natives cultivating the fields, and good specimens of native industries, in the form of silks, cloths, pottery, etc. In front of the museum is the famous gun Zamzama, a huge piece brought from Kabul. It is mounted upon a strong wooden carriage, heavily bound with iron. I believe the natives are greatly attached to it.

The railway workshops are very extensive, and the company has provided substantial houses for its employees, with a good swimming bath, library, billiard room, theatre and recreation grounds—all for their exclusive use.

I turn back to-morrow and will probably reach Delhi on 15th, passing over, on my return trip, the same line I came by ; but as it will be daylight, over parts of the country that the upcoming train makes at night, I shall probably find something new and interesting. I shall see the beds of the large rivers Beas and Sutlej, both comparatively dry at this seaon, but indicating from their wide and sandy beds the enormous volumes of water that must flow down them in the rainy season and after the snows in the Himalaya mountains begin melting.

XI

SOLDIERING IN INDIA.

HEADQRS. GEN. SIR F. ROBERTS, NEAR DELHI,
January 20th, 1886.

I REACHED this camp on the 15th inst., where, thanks to "The Chief" and his military secretary, Col. Pole-Carew, of the Coldstreams, I was furnished with a most comfortable tent, and also one of the "A" pattern for my servant; the "A" somewhat larger than that used in our Service—say about twelve by fifteen feet, a little higher, and with a small wall of eighteen inches, and lined with yellow cotton cloth. I am thus particular, as it is the identical field-tent used by the enlisted men of the Indian army.

Usually, in hot weather, this has the addition of a " fly," which gives an air-space between it and the body of the tent, and adds to its coolness. The slight wall when raised, admits the passage of a current of air. The cavalry use a similar tent, but about double the depth, and intended for a great number of men.

As for my own canvas home, it is almost palatial. Imagine two conical-roofed tents with square walls, one within the other, and supported by a single pole through the centre, the interior space being about twenty-four feet square; walls some six and a half to seven feet high, the outer tent walls somewhat higher and separated from the inner by a space of three feet.   Each tent has four doors, which roll up, and an additional protection of a green blind made of light bamboo ; both inner and outer tents being lined with colored cotton cloth, generally of yellow ground, and agreeable to the eyes.

The accredited foreign officers have still larger tents, mostly hipped roofs, provided with fire-places, and divided by canvas partitions, their fronts and approaches to the entrances made bright and cheerful by pots of tropical plants.   In truth, everything has been done to render their visit agreeable, and no pains spared to enable them to have a thorough insight of the material, organization, and inner working of the Indian army.

During the manœuvres they were provided with a flying camp, where every reasonable comfort was arranged.   In truth, I believe they had a dinner party nearly every night while in the field.

Before dismissing the subject of tents, I wish to note some of the still larger—as, for instance, the reception and dining tents of the commander-in-chief.

In the former, at an evening party in honor of the Viceroy, Earl Dufferin, I saw some two hundred guests, and have dined with General Roberts when there were at least forty at table. The headquarters' mess-tent, which was at my service, could dine, readily, forty-five. English officers make a good deal of their mess, and rarely dine save in the prescribed uniform, which is a mess-jacket, rather elaborately embroidered and a vest that is richly decorated.

My tent is but a few yards from the mess-tent, and its annex the reception tent, which has an open wood-fire, and serves as an excellent lounging place, when not more profitably employed. I was invited to join, and paid the regular initiation fee of five rupees. Three rather luxurious meals are served each day for the moderate sum of five rupees—about $2.00. The hours as established are : Breakfast from 8:30 to 10 A. M., lunch from 1 to 3 P.M., and dinner at 8 P. M. Colonel Keyser, of the Royal Fusiliers, has undertaken the mess duties, and is a most genial and popular man, as also an intelligent and efficient officer.

Most of the gentlemen, I'm here thrown with, are of considerable rank, and have been, from their peculiar fitness, selected from various regiments and sections of India to perform duty at headquarters during the " Camp of Exercise,"—such as umpires in the various engagements in the field, signal services, etc , Colonel Keyser has the Signal Department.

But to return to the rank and file of the Service. The native troops struck me, and I believe our accredited officers are equally impressed, as being far in advance of what was looked for, the Ghoorkas and Sikhs being especially noticeable—the latter from their good height, fine physique, intelligence, and general fondness for the Service. They were among the last of the native tribes to yield to British rule, but have ever since been the most loyal of Her Majesty's Indian subjects. They were thoroughly devoted during the Mutiny of 1857, and did good service against the rebels. Their stronghold is about Amritzar, a city near Lahore, where they have one of their most sacred temples, known as the Golden Temple. The Ghoorkas come from Nipaul, in the Himalayas, and show much more of the Mongolian type of feature. They are rather short, but a natty-looking set of men, armed, in addition to their rifle, with a large, curved sheath-knife, which is worn on the belt. They are said to be unrelenting, and rarely spare the life of even a fallen foe.

Nipaul is an independent province on the borders of Oude, but I understand there is no serious objection to recruiting for the English Service.

The Guides are a fine body of cavalry, the men for which are almost entirely recruited on the northern and northwestern frontier. The Putans also furnish a share of the rank and file, but I am not fully informed as to their native district.

The field uniform of all arms of the Service is made of a material called *karkee*. It is a species of American duck of yellowish clay color, and consists of a jacket, short trousers, and a pair of leggings called "putties," a roll of cloth wound around the leg in a spiral form from the ankle to the knee, in a manner similar to that in which race horses' legs are bandaged.

For full dress the native as well as the European troops wear the tunic of various colors and of different facings. Red is still the prevailing color, but in conversation with officers, I gathered the impression that the karkee color, or drab, is the one which many favor, as it so nearly approaches that of the soil, as to make the soldiers almost indistinguishable ; and I observed that when in the field, except for the turban which the natives wear at all times, it was difficult to discover a body of troops, especially if they were not on the march. The European soldier also wears his *'topc* or sun-hat with the karkee, and is less observable than the native. The Ghoorkas are an exception, and do not wear the turban, but in its stead a species of skull-cap, not unlike the jaunty head piece of the English soldier, with whom, by-the-by, he fraternizes more than any other of the native troops.

He drinks whiskey and associates more freely · with " Tommy Atkins " than any other native, and I have heard that he imitates him in the use of strong language. I observed that the *Chief* had him as guard in front of his and the tents of his personal staff, which rather argues that he is a favorite in that quarter.

The method of pay and subsistence of the native troops forms a feature of the Indian Service that is worthy of notice. The cavalry recruit brings with him either his own horse or two hundred rupees (a rupee is supposed to be worth about forty cents, but it is at present greatly depreciated), and his colonel prefers the rupees, as he can mount the man on a horse of government selection, generally on one of the animals imported from New South Wales, and usually termed " walers." Should he have neither horse nor money, the two hundred rupees are charged against him, and paid off in monthly instalments. His monthly pay differs in the different Presidencies, but averages about twenty-eight rupees. On this he must subsist himself, purchasing his food from the natives, and, as he rarely eats meat, his wants are readily satisfied. He must also pay for the services of a grass-cutter, as one grass-cutter is allowed to two horses, and he also pays the grain contractor for the necessary short forage required for his horse.

The infantryman's pay averages about seven rupees per month, on which he must subsist himself and provide his own cooks. Even the rough quarters of a cantonment for the native troops is paid for from the soldier's allowance, and as garrisons are changed they are appraised, and the incoming troops required to take them at valuation. It will be seen that the native gives far less trouble than "Tommy Atkins," as the European soldier is usually styled. I was induced to ask how the latter got his cognomen, so generally in use. and learned that it came from the printed forms used in the English Service being signed " T. Atkins." There is a certain allowance of clothing made to all native troops on enlistment, which is afterward kept from their pay.

One of the features of this command, that is especially striking to an American, is its elephant battery of heavy guns, which I took the pains to examine quite minutely There were really two kinds of draught, the elephant and the bullock, there being eighteen of the former and three hundred of the latter. The wheel-elephant is placed in a pair of wide shafts, and has a very large, heavy, and strong saddle, not unlike a huge cart-saddle. This is attached by a heavy leathern band and iron chains to the shafts. He has also a strong breast-strap and breeching. The lead elephant is hitched in a similar manner to that in which the lead horse in a tandem team would be. The bullocks accompany the battery not only for draught purposes, for which they use from four to six yokes to each gun, but because they are indispensible in time of action, as the elephant will not stand fire. He, realizing the danger, would be liable to stampede the guns, and hence is detached when the enemy is near, and bullocks yoked in. There were some superb specimens of the latter attached to the battery. There were also two or three mountain batteries, in which the guns and parts of carriages were on the backs of mules. I did not see any very fine specimens of the latter, and don't think there are any, particularly when viewed from an American standpoint, as I believe we have the finest mules in the world. Both the horse-and field-artilery looked well, and the batteries are in the hands of efficient and intelligent commanders. Since the Mutiny of 1857 none but Europeans have been used for this service.

Not the least interesting or noticeable feature of this Indian Service is the great attention given to manly sports and exercises. Every opportunity is furnished for the development of physique and for acquiring skill in the amusements, in which the most daring and probably the most popular is tent-pegging. This consists in riding at full tilt and taking, with the lance a rather short and broad tent-peg from the ground ; and you may be a little surprised when I tell you that Gen. Roberts led off in this sport, and with his team of four made the best score of the season. There were numerous other mounted and foot sports, such as lance against sword, sword against bayonet, sword against sword, bayonet against bayonet, tent-pegging with sword, cutting lemons with sword, tug of war, foot racing, and acrobatic and gymnastic feats, and also pony and camel races.

The latter, while very novel, did not develop any very great speed, and I hardly think, at any time in the course, exceeded more than eight miles per hour; thus disposing of the repeated assertion of the novelist, who frequently likens the fleetness of the camel to that of the wind.

The "march past" of the entire force, some 35,000, closed the Camp of Exercise. It was done in the midst of a pouring rain. By the time the cavalry and horse, and foot, artillery had passed the reviewing point, the dark soil had been churned into the consistency of a bed of thin mortar, and when the native infantry came by, many of whom wore only the slipper, there was a sad loss of this rather necessary appendage of the foot soldier, and I rather think this test may bring about a change. All troops, native as well as European, marched by with great precision, and the line and dress of the double companies—we style them divisions—were admirably observed.

As the elephant battery passed, the knowing animals raised their trunks and saluted, for which purpose they folded the trunk into the form of the letter S, holding it square to the front.

The appearance of the ground, in and about the slight mound where the reviewing officer was posted, calls for some attention, as it was made up of all sorts and conditions of men, from those who were in the handsome four-in-hand with native out-riders, to the humble peasant who had trudged out five miles to see the grand parade. There were all sorts of mounts, but chiefly noticeable were the camels and elephants. I counted seventy-five of the latter, many richly caparisoned and provided with howdahs for carrying the families of chiefs. The sight was truly Eastern, as all the natives were in holiday attire, and the gaudy colors of their dresses made the assembly all the more picturesque.

I was a little disappointed in the number of important native chiefs, Maharaja Scindia, Raja of Gwalior, Maharaja of Kutch Behar, Maharaja of Jodhpur, Maharaja of Ulwar, Maharaja of Nadir, being all of any great importance that I heard of as being on the ground. The native contingents, however, were out in considerable force, and, although the last to march past, made a very respectable appearance.

Although the Camp of Exercise virtually closed with the review and "march past" given to the Viceroy on the 19th, yet the troops remained in camp for the purpose of drying their equipments and uniforms and also to take part in the various sports. The accredited officers take their departure to-morrow night, and are to wind up their visit by sight-seeing

in various parts of India, at government expense.
I think they must be pleased with their reception, as
everything possible has been done to render their
stay agreeable. I enclose the speech of the Viceroy welcoming them to India, which strikes me as
particularly happy.

*   *   *   *   *   *   *

"Again, on the other side are two officers whose
presence here is as grateful to my feelings as that of
any of their colleagues, inasmuch as they represent
the Army of the United States, a country which I
had often occasion·to visit when Governor-General
of Canada, and whose border I never passed without
experiencing at the hands of its inhabitants such an
amount of kindness and hospitality as it would be im-
possible for me to forget."

*   *   *   *   *   *

Before closing I wish to add my testimony to the
personal magnetism of General Roberts, the Commander-in-Chief. I listened to the brief and extem-
poraneous dinner speech welcoming the foreign officers, and it seemed so happy, so easily delivered,
and so telling, that I regretted seeing him sit down.
He is known among the troops as " Our Bobs," and
I can readily understand how it is that I hear from
every quarter that they are greatly attached and
ready to go wherever he leads.

Previous to dismissing the subject of the Camp of
Exercise I wish to bear testimony to the universal

kindness and hospitality that I enjoyed from every one I was thrown in contact with, but I desire, particularly, to thank Brigr. General Luck and Colonel Heyland, First Bengal Lancers, both of whom were most kind and attentive.

I leave this camp to-morrow afternoon for Agra and other points further to the eastward, and it's possible, if I find anything that I think may interest you, you may hear from me again.   *   *   *   *   *

XII.

DELHI TO AGRA.

LAURIE'S HOTEL, AGRA, TEMP. IN SHADE, 62°.
January 27th, 1886.

REALISING that there would be a crowd at the railway station, I left camp quite early in the morning of the 21st, and arrived some two hours in advance of the starting of the train from Delhi, but it was only by the best of good luck that I got my baggage weighed and was able to get aboard the train. Such utter confusion and want of system I've rarely ever witnessed. It seemed to demonstrate that native employees, while working in a regular routine, are equal to the task, but the moment they are unusually pressed, by heavy traffic, they break down completely. This is not the only complaint. I've heard that several others expressed themselves more decidedly and in more forcible language than I have given. However, I did get away and, although a little late, reached this hotel after a pleasant journey of some six hours, early in the evening, and I am most comfortably lodged. It is one of the best inns I've yet found in India.

And now, where and how shall I begin to describe the many and highly interesting objects of this city—the seat of Moslem architecture during the best building period of the great Mogul kings? It was some twenty miles from this city, at Futhepoor Sikri that the great Ackbar began his first permanent residence—selecting for the site a commanding ridge, which he enclosed with a strong wall, flanked by towers and pierced for musketry. The remains, still standing, indicate the immense labor that was performed. In this stronghold were placed the sacred mosque, the residence of his favorite wives and his own palace, with its adjuncts of baths, etc., and stables for horses, camels and elephants, together with an immense palace for his guests.

All the buildings are of permanent material—being either of marble or red sandstone—quarries of the latter abounding a few miles from Futhepoor. The residences of his wives are interesting places to visit, showing that, in spite of his Moslem faith, he was sufficiently liberal to think that there were other creeds that he could accept, and that he permitted his Hindoo wife to practice her religion is evidenced from the character of her home, which displays not only the Hindoo architecture in various forms, but has numerous shrines devoted to Hindoo gods.

The home of Mariam, or Marie Begam, his Christian wife, is a small house of red sandstone, rather simple in its style, and devoid of ornamentation, except some frescoes, now much defaced, showing that the subjects were taken from the Scriptures. She is said to have been a Portuguese, which is not at all improbable, as they were residents in the country at an early period. Whether this tradition be correct or not, I must acknowledge to have greatly enjoyed there the lunch we took with us from Agra, as the building is now used as a place of refreshment, and our servants spread the table in what is now called, " Mariam's House."

One of the most interesting relics of the past is the shrine of Shekh Salim Chisti, a faithful priest of Ackbar's reign, and who, tradition relates, furnished a son and heir to the throne in the person of Jahangir. The tomb is a beautiful specimen of Oriental work in pure white marble, and the marble screen which encloses the sarcophagus is one of the finest specimens of the kind to be found in India. The number of geometrical figures of which it is composed, is marvelous, and it would require hours to work them all out, so completely do they run into each other. The brackets which support the projecting roof of this shrine are particularly noticeable—being similar in style to those over the entrances to many of the Hindoo temples I've seen. Visitors to the exhibition in London, to be held, I believe in April, will see some excellent specimens of them, as I saw them being packed at the studios of the best sculptors in Agra.

Our guide, through the remains of the royal residence of Futhepoor Sikri was a bright looking lad of fourteen, whom his grandfather introduced to us as a direct descendant of some royal blood that I'll not attempt to record. He was ready with his tongue, and when I asked him for his name he wrote it out correctly, thus, "Walyooddeen" and he further insisted upon taking us to the school where he had acquired his English, and we were detained some time in listening to the boy's reading. As a bit of family news he stated that "he had been married one month but would not see his wife 'till next year," so little have the youth of the country to say in reference to their first marriage.

We passed, on our return to Agra, a most gorgeous wedding procession, made up of friends and relatives on foot, in carriages and in bullock carts. There was also an attempt at a band, in which the native drum, a barrel shaped affair, on which the drummer made much noise, played a prominent part. Two or three gorgeous imitations of elephants were also borne in the procession. We stopped and asked to see the groom, who was brought in the arms of an old man. The child's apparel—for he was not more than six or seven years old—was very gaudy, and his neck

TOMB OF THE GREAT AKBAR, SIKANDARAH.

and arms were covered with silver jewelry, which I handled and admired. This attention the child evidently enjoyed. The bride was in a closed palanquin, and we did not see her, but I was told that she was even younger. This is called, I believe the first marriage (we would style it betrothal), but I understand the marriage is not consummated until the girl is twelve and the boy is fourteen years of age.

The tomb of Ackbar the Great is located at Sikandarah, some four or five miles from Agra. To this we devoted a special pilgrimage, and were well repaid. The mausoleum occupies the centre of a large garden, which is enclosed with a heavy wall. I liked exceedingly the appearance of the grounds which are dotted over with fine, large trees, with here and there some bright-colored climbing plant like the Bouqainvillea and honey-suckle to give life to the scene. The space enclosed must cover several acres. Its walks are overgrown, but some of the roads are well kept up. You enter this through a massive gateway of red sandstone, on which are inscriptions taken from the Koran. It is of great height, and the views from its upper platform are very fine and comprehensive. At each angle rises a marble minaret of two stories. Two of them have their upper stories knocked off. I believe this vandalism is charged to the Jats. Who they were, or now are, I don't at present know. The mausoleum itself is an imposing building of red sandstone and of several stories. In a gloomy vault beneath lies all that remains of this great leader and ruler. Ascending the building to the fourth platform, you reach the white marble corridor which enclosed the cenotaph of Ackbar. It is a beautiful block of white marble, totally unadorned or uninscribed, for his works and deeds needed no recording ; they spoke for themselves. The outside lattice work (in marble) of the corridor is exquisitely done, and the squares of which it is made up are each of a different pattern. We lingered a long time at this elevation, viewing Jumna, the fort at Agra, and the Taj Mahal, in the distance, and the scene was a beautiful one.

Having given some account of the interesting objects, in the suburbs of Agra I must attempt to tell you of the attractions of the city itself..

So much of beauty and so much of interest centres in and about .Agra that it is difficult to decide at what point to begin describing what is to be seen. Perhaps the best plan is to follow the order in which I saw it myself, be it right or wrong.

Murray recommends the traveler to see the Taj Mahal (or Taj, as it is more frequently called) as often as possible during his stay, and this plan I followed—going there immediately after my arrival in this city, and by the road constructed during the famine of 1838. By this route you come directly upon this beautiful mausoleum without catching

glimpses here and there. At least, that was my experience. I entered the grand south gate—and here
I must stop a moment and admire this beautiful work
of red sandstone, some 140 feet high by 110 wide,
and having its inner face inlaid with ornaments and
inscriptions from the Koran, and the under side of
its large dome covered with geometrical figures in
white marble. It is certainly a most fitting entrance
to the superb structure beyond, and were it not
placed so near the latter would receive far greater
attention. Passing through this, I came suddenly
into a beautiful garden, with the Taj immediately in
front of me, as it is at the end of a broad avenue,
having a pretty lake in the middle portion and rich
tropical foliage on either border. I involuntarily
stopped and for many moments could do nothing
more than admire this pearly white mausoleum so
admirably placed, and so aided by its surroundings
as to give me the most beautiful impressions ever
made by any work of man. I saw it repeatedly afterward—by moonlight, when its interior was illumin-
ated, and from every possible point—but from none
did it please so well as when viewed from the great
south gate. In my haste to tell my impressions of
this superb work—the most beautiful in India and
possibly in the world. I have failed to give its origin
or enumerate some of its proportions. The work is
a labor of love and affection, and was built by Shah
Jahan, the fifth in the order of succession, of the great

Mogul kings, who reigned from 1627 to 1658, as a tomb for his favorite Queen, Mumtaz Mahal, which freely translated, means "Pride of the Palace." There is a love story in connection with this marriage, which can be appropriately introduced here:

It seems that in early life Shah Jahan fell desperately in love with Mumtaz, but from reasons of state was forbidden to marry her, and another bride was selected for him. After ascending the throne he again sought her out, and, finding her a widow, renewed his devotion and speedily made her Queen— and she was truly a Queen and helpmate. So much did he realize this that he directed her image to be stamped on the coin of the realm alongside his own, and consulted her in all important State affairs. The following description is condensed from Ferguson, and will give the reader an admirable and correct idea of its proportions :

"The enclosure includes an inner and outer court, the entire width of which is about one fifth of a mile, and extends along the banks of the Jumna River some 500 yards. The mausoleum stands above the level of the eye, on a double terrace—the first of red sandstone twenty feet high and a thousand broad, at the extremities of which stand two mosques, of some dark stone, facing each other ; midway between rises the second terrace of marble, fifteen feet high and three hundred feet square, on the corners of which are four round, tapering minarets. In the centre of all stands the Taj, of pure white marble, its large central dome rising nearly 200 feet above the pavement below. The mausoleum is a square of 186 feet, with its corners cut off. Four smaller marble domes rise about these truncated angles. The tombs of Shah Jahan and Mumtaz Mahall lie immediately beneath the central dome, and are surrounded by an exquisite marble screen, made up of geometrical figures. The tombs are inlaid with some rare stones arranged in floral designs, and have escaped almost entirely the ravages which one finds in the royal tombs elsewhere in India."

I hope I've conveyed some idea of this beautiful work ; if not, all I can say to your readers is, that if they have the leisure and wish to pass a winter away from the frosts and snows of our latitude, they should take a ticket for India, and I'm sure they would get their reward.

Let us now proceed to the Fort of Agra, which contained the royal residence, or palace, the private and public audience halls, the family mosque and several private mosques ; the treasury, etc. It is a strong work, with its walls and flanking defenses of red sandstone. It has an imposing effect, its walls being 70 feet high, pierced for musketry at most points, and its projecting portions arranged for artillery. The ditch is thirty feet wide, and opposite the main entrance is a most formidable and well-proportioned work of red sandstone that would have made the storming of the fort almost a hopeless task.

One of the first objects of our visit was " The Moti Masjid," or " Pearl Mosque," an account of which I take from Bayard Taylor, whose great enthusiasm, added to his superb command of language, well fitted him to give the following glowing description :

" This is the Moti Masjid, or Pearl Mosque, as it is poetically termed. It is in truth the pearl of all mosques—of small dimensions, but absolutely perfect in style and proportion. It is lifted on a lofty sandstone platform, and from without nothing can be seen but its three domes of white marble and gilded spires. In all distant views of the fort these domes are seen like silvery bubbles which have rested a moment on its walls, and which the next breeze will sweep away. Ascending a long flight of steps, a heavy door was opened for me, and I stood in the court yard of the mosque, on its eastern side, and the pure blue of the sky overhead. The three domes crown a corridor and open towards the court, and are divided in three aisles by a triple row of the most exquisitely proportioned Saracenic arches. The Moti Masjid can be compared to no other edifice that I have ever seen. To my eye it is absolutely perfect. While its architecture is the purest Saracenic, which some suppose cannot exist without an ornament, it has he severe simplicity of Doric art. It has, in fact, nothing which can properly be called ornament. It is a sanctuary so pure and stainless, revealing so exalted a spirit of worship, that I felt humbled, as a Christian, to think that our noble religion has never inspired its architects to surpass this temple to God and Mahomed."

In spite of all he has said, it did not impress me as did the Pearl Mosque at Delhi. Perhaps that was my fault, or perhaps because one can't repeat so often the sense of the beautiful, especially when the first impression has been so vivid.

The Diwanji Khas, or private audincee hall, is one of the gems of the fort. It was here that the Emperor gave audience to his chief princes. Composed of white marble, it has some fine carving, and the columns supporting the Saracenic arches, are decorated with floral designs of inlaid marble and precious stones, the red carnelion being conspicuous. The view from the terrace in front of it is one of the finest about Agra, and takes in the River Jumna, which runs close to the base of the fort wall, the residence and garden across the river, including a glimpse of the beautiful tomb, in white marble, of I'timadu 'd daulah, and down the stream, about a mile away, the superb Taj. I made frequent visits to the fort, but never failed to mount this terrace, especially at sunset, when the scene from it was sometimes gorgeous. I usually met there, and also at the Taj, Mrs. Taylor, wife of an English Colonel, who was filling her portfolio with choice bits of Agra's best works.

There are many other points of interest about this old city, but I can't enumerate them all.

A morning visit to the Agra jail was an interesting one. There are some 1,500 inmates at present—about 1,000 less than usual. Great neatness was displayed in every portion, and I should judge from their healthy appearance, that the prisoners were well cared for. The looms where the famous Agra carpets are made were especially interesting. These carpets are all hand made, and are of heavy texture. Each loom has its "reader," who sings out the colors from a pattern before him. These readers were uunsually bright-looking lads of 12 to 14 years. Most of the looms were engaged in making carpets for the Indian exhibit, to be held in London this Spring. Of the foreign houses that patronize this establishment I observed that the *Magazin du Louvre*, at Paris, was the heaviest purchaser.

I leave Agra with regret, and with the feeling that there are many beauties that I have not fully looked into, but possibly this may be for good and the means of tempting me back to India, for it is the Mecca of this Eastern land, which all travelers eventually reach, as about it centers more and richer specimens of Moslem architecture during its best period than in any other portion of India.

Before closing my letter I think it but fair to enumerate the great Mogul kings and give the date of their control of this portion of India:

Baber reigned from 1526 to 1530; Humayun from 1530 to 1556; Ackbar from 1556 to 1605; Jehangir from 1605 to 1627; Shah Jehan from 1627 to 1658; Aurungzeb from 1658 to 1707.

The greatest builder—the one who displayed the highest and most delicate taste—was Shah Jehan.

A comparison of these dates with those of the most active rulers of Western Europe, such as Henry VIII. and Queen Elizabeth, of England, Francis I. and Charles V., of Continental Europe, shows that while the latter were making history in their respective lands the Moslem Kings of India were not idle.

XIII.

AGRA TO BENARES.

CLARK'S HOTEL,
HOLY HINDOO CITY OF BENARES,
January 31st, 1886.

COMING directly from Agra to this old city does not add either to its beauty or attractiveness, as the traveler, who has found so much of grace and beauty in the works of the Mogul kings, feels rather disappointed at the stiff and contracted style of the Hindoo temples. The very best I've seen consist only of an outer court of rather narrow dimensions, with the main building in the centre, and rising from it is the pyramidal-shaped tower, which is always the chief feature. The exterior of this tower is usually elaborately decorated with a variety of images, among which are all sorts of animals, such as the elephant, cow, monkey, etc., and also a number of human figures. I've never attempted to master their mythology hence I am supremely ignorant of the meaning of all these, and only know that they enter into, or are a part of, their religion.

The Golden Temple at Amritzar is an exception to the above rather disparaging comments, but it is so beautifully placed—being in the centre of a pretty lake, bordered by a marble pavement—and of a style of architecture so strongly resembling the Moslem, that I at first mistook it for a Mahommedan edifice, so that I hardly class it among the Hindoo works.

Still, I am glad to be here, and can recall that as a boy, while studying the map of India, that Benares had a mysterious attraction that I've not forgotten. The East India Railway line does not bring you directly to the city, but one changes at a station about half a hour from this, and you come down by a branch road—crossing the Ganges on a bridge of boats. You have still a drive of four miles before reaching this very comfortable hotel—one of the very best I've met with. There is a home, cottage-like look about it that indicates both comfort and neatness. All the archways to the various apartments are draped with morning glories, and the entire grounds or space within the enclosure (here called compound) are kept scrupulously neat and clean, and Mrs. Clark's flower garden, although limited in extent, can boast many very handsome and choice roses. The interior of the hotel is alike cozy and home-like, and as an English lady remarked to me: "It's quite like a nice country hotel at home."

One of my first visits was to the Durga Temple—generally called by Europeans the "Monkey Tem-

ple." On our way to it we passed the "Car of Jur-
ganaut," an immense affair on some dozen or more
wheels. A large platform, with a canopy above it,
forms the upper portion of the car, which I presume
the idols occupied in the course of the procession. I
believe this car is still used in some of their ceremonies, but it is scrupulously guarded by the police to
prevent fanatics from throwing themselves under the
wheels.

As we neared the Monkey Temple I stopped the
carriage at a fruit stand and purchased some sweets
and fruits to give the monkeys. These creatures approached us slyly and grabbed our offerings in a most
animal-like way, and then ran off to devour them.

The temple is surrounded by a number of large
trees, in the hollows of which the monkeys live. This
temple, which is stained red with ochre, stands in
the centre of a quadrangle, and near the entrance is
a band stand, where the priests beat a large drum
three times each day. A sacrificial stone, also near
the entrance, had its upper part and base covered
with blood, showing that some animal had recently
been offered up to propitiate the gods.

The number of temples in this city is enormous,
and they are met with at nearly every turn, and new
ones are in course of erection. I visited two or three
more —such as the "Golden Temple" and "Cow Temple," and then gave up the job. In the latter I found a
number of Hindoo cows, which are regarded as sa-

cred. They looked fat and sleek, and were chewing their cuds like ordinary animals of their class.

One of the most interesting mornings that I've passed was on the river Ganges at the early hour of 7 A. M , when the residents and pilgrims are engaged in bathing and saying their prayers. Surgeon Genl. and Mrs. Webb, English Army, kindly invited me to join their party for this excursion. Starting well up the river, we floated down stream, past the various palaces and ghats, (or steps) in front of them, where there were large numbers of bathers, and also past the burning ghat, where the bodies are cremated. The process was not in operation, but a body on a bier was brought down and placed in the Ganges while awaiting the preparation of the funeral pile. The pilgrims to whom I've alluded form a very large element in the population of the city, and one encounters them everywhere in the streets—usually accompanied by bearers, who carry two earthen jars at the end of a bamboo pole—one containing the ashes of some deceased relative, whichis to be cast into the sacred river and the other designed to carry a away supply of the holy water from the Ganges. Another and noticeable feature of our morning's visit to the river was the number of priests that we saw along the river bank, seated upon raised platforms and expounding in Hindustani passages from the Sanskrit. Their audiences were chiefly made up of women, who were squatting in front of them.

We stopped near one of the assemblages and watched for some time the speaker, who was round both in face and figure. His gesticulations and facial expressions were marked. I was disposed to think them comical, and we fancied that on our approach he raised his voice and directed his explanations at us unbelievers, but I regret to say that his eloquence was entirely lost on me. I believe Mrs. Webb, who has been some years in the country, was able to understand some of his remarks. As we were returning to our carriage a priest, with his little pots of colored earth and the stamps with which the good Hindoo has his forehead marked, stopped us and asked us to witness the opération of marking, which we did. He then asked for backshish, but as Mrs. B. expressed a wish to possess these stamps, in place of backshish I gave him a small sum and carried away the sacred seals. As these marks denote the caste of the wearer, I should go into a further explanation of their meaning, but I respectfully decline— it being a subject beyond my comprehension. Various explanations have been given by different writers as to the origin of caste and its meanings, but beyond knowing that it indicates various grades in social life, I positively can tell nothing. I recall that shortly after my arrival at the Byculla Club, at Bombay, I asked a most intelligent member if he had in any way mastered the subject of caste, and his reply was; "I've been now more than thirty years in the country, and know scarcely anything of it."

I don't think I've alluded in any previous letters to the social status of women, and may as well introduce the subject here. Nothing is more striking than the entire exclusion of women from all vocations which are likely to bring her in contact with strangers or others than members of her own family. One never meets them in the hotels, private houses, shops — or, in truth, anywhere. All your wants at a hotel are supplied by men, and even your washwoman, or "Dhobi," is a man, and my linen is standing proof that he has been a vigorous one, and shows in a most lamentable form the effects of pounding the articles upon stones the usual method of washing in this country.

Another excursion that I found very agreeable was to the palace of the Maharaja of Benares, which is located on the opposite side of the river from the city. A drive of some three miles brought us to the banks of the river, which we crossed in a native boat, and then walked up the bank to the entrance of the palace. I sent in my card, which was promptly acknowledged, and an intelligent secretary of the Maharaja accompanied me through the audience room and one or two reception rooms. There was nothing very remarkable about them — their furniture being of modern European styles. The portraits of the various members of the royal family were the most interesting subjects that I saw, and which the secretary explained. We were shown, also, the howdah and trappings of the elephants, some of which were rich and expensive ; but the great charm of the place was the fine view one gets from the balconies, of the city and the river, which flows at the base of the castle walls. The river is navigable for light-draught steamers, even up to Allahabad, but since the introduction of the railway they have almost entirely disappeared.

As I propose mailing this at Calcutta, I'll leave off writing for the present.

Spencer's Hotel, Calcutta, February 3d, 1886.—The ride from Benares to this city, by the East India Railway, proved an interesting one. Leaving that city about midday, we reached the terminus, Howrah, as it is called, on the opposite side of the Hoogly River from this city, at six o'clock in the morning of the following day ; time, about 18 hours; distance 360 miles. This is by the mail or fast train. All other trains are far slower, and make innumerable stops. The first-class carriages of this line—and they may be taken as samples of most roads—are very roomy and rather comfortable—each compartment containing two long sofas that are nicely upholstered, and two hanging shelves, all of which can be converted into beds at night, but it is seldom that the upper berths are required. There is attached to each compartment a toilet room, but every traveler must supply his own bedding, and hence a pillow and a roll of wraps become an essential part of nearly every Indian traveler's outfit. as most all the fast trains start from the chief points at night.

Shortly after leaving Benares we entered the largest opium growing district of India, and at Patna passed its chief shipping point. Fortunately, I fell in with a very intelligent engineer, who explained the mode of preparing the drug. It is only the white flowered poppy that is grown, and the fields were in a mass of bloom. It seems that the bulb of the plant, containing the seeds, upon being scratched exudes a gummy substance, which is carefully collected. This bulb is worked at until all the gum is exhausted. The aggregate of various collections is then heated, and its watery particles driven off. The residue is collected in two-pound balls, enclosed in the poppy leaves, and is then ready for market. Of course, this is only a rough description, as great care is necessary, in driving off the water, not to exceed a certain temperature, and experts are employed in the preparation of the drug. I have seen in the course of my few days' stay here, many cart loads of this pernicious drug on its way to the Government warehouses, from whence it is shipped by a special line of steamers (known as the opium line) to China and elsewhere. What a pity that a great Government like that of England should be engaged in encouraging the growth of this article, for it does encourage its growth and to that end often advances the farmer the necessary funds. It also designates the amount of

soil that shall be cultivated, and all this that it may
secure the paltry sum of $15,000,000 towards its
India revenue. I don't wonder that the thinking and
philanthropic spirits of London are holding meetings
and endeavoring to bring about a different order of
things.

Near *Patna* there is a branch line of this road that
runs southward almost to *Buddha Gay*, a pilgrimage to which I should have made, as it is of great
interest from being the spot related by Buddha, for
his long fast and meditation. Murray quoting from
high authority states that " it continued through
six years, and that he began by living on a plum
a day, then on a grain of rice, then on a
grain of sesum, and then he took nothing." It contains a handsome temple, and many interesting objects connected with the early life of this great
teacher, whose disciples far out-number any other
faith on the globe.

From this point he went to Benares, where he first
preached; hence both places are sacred to the faithful Buddhist.

XIV.

CALCUTTA TO DARJEELING.

WOODLAND HOTEL, DARJEELING,
7,300 FEET ABOVE THE SEA.
TEMP. IN SHADE AT SUNRISE, 32°.
February 5th, 1886.

MY excursion to this mountain resort and sanitarium for the troops and residents of Calcutta has been not only successful, but most interesting. Darjeeling is one of those points that 'the tourist does not care to leave out; yet, as it requires nearly four days from Calcutta to go and return, with a possibility of making the mountain section of the journey in a fog, and not even getting a glimpse of the snow peaks he is in search of, it requires some little determination to face these posssible disappointments. Happily I've accomplished the journey under the most favorable of skies and have been rewarded by seeing the tallest mountain peaks in the world—the highest, Mount Everest, being 29,002 feet, and having as neighbors Kinchinjunga, 28,156 feet; Janu, 25,304 feet; Kabru, 24,015 feet, and others. I might add to the list, but this will suffice to give you an idea of the enormous altitude to which the highest peaks of the Himalaya range attain. The excursion, as made from Calcutta, can be accomplished entirely by rail. The first portion, over the level country lying between the Hoogly and Ganges, is made by the Eastern Bengal State Railway, of five-foot gauge. After crossing the Ganges you take the Northern Bengal State Railway, of the metre gauge, and the last, or mountain section, is traveled by the Darjeeling Himalayan Railway, of two-feet gauge. The country passed over is in the main densely populated, and we saw along the line most extensive fields of various kinds of grain, prominent among them being barley, which is rapidly matured and will be cut within thirty days. Sugar cane is also grown to a considerable extent, and we saw numerous camps where the natives were grinding it and converting the juice into sugar. There were, beside, a number of other grains in various stages of advancement.

As we approached the mountains the native villages showed a different style of architecture, and in place of the mud huts, so common in the Northern and Middle sections of India, we found their homes largely constructed of bamboo, which grows in great luxuriance and attains immense size. They use sections of the bamboo at Darjeeling for milk cans.

The roofs of their houses are closely thatched, and are constructed with a curved ridge not unlike a hog's back, and with long, descending eaves—carrying off readily the heavy rains to which the region is subject, and protecting the walls of the cottages. There were no evidences of irrigation, and I infer that they have ample water for all crops.

The peculiar form of roof that I've attempted to describe especially attracted my attention—not only from its rather odd, yet graceful appearance, but also because I had seen its counterpart in the roofs of the various " Audience Halls" in and about Delhi and Lahore, as constructed under the Mogul kings; and I'm quite of the opinion that the builder in stone and marble, recognizing the graceful shape, borrowed the idea from the native hut of this region.

Before leaving the " Eastern Bengal line " I must speak of a cast-iron sleeper I noticed, which is gradually replacing the wooden one. and as all the world is interested in finding a good substitute for wood, I'll attempt to describe it.   Under each rail is placed a cast-iron disk about three feet long and fifteen inches wide ; these are connected transversely by an iron rod.   Each of the disks has a permanent cheek, cast with it, that rests snugly against the outer face of the rail.   There is also a movable cheek for each rail, that rests against the inner face, through which the transverse rod runs.   By means of a wedge driven through a slot in this movable cheek and the transverse bar all is made snug and firm. The simplicity of the various parts, and the facility with which they are laid down, seemed to commend the system and struck me as being quite worthy of notice. I questioned an intelligent engineer connected with the public works of India, and whom I met on the train. He stated that the system had been very thoroughly tested, and he believed in its permanent usefulness. The wooden sleeper in this country is very short-lived, owing to the dry-rot. It has also an enemy in the white ant, which eats it up.

We reached the mountain section of our journey early in the morning, and, as the sky was beautifully clear, caught a glimpse of the Himalayan snows in the far distance. Besides, we were assured, by the Assistant Superintendent of the line, that we would have fine weather, and all indications pointed in that direction. The tiny cars and engine which made up our last train were amusing to look at; still we found them quite equal to the work required, and they took us up the mountains in a very comfortable way.

The line follows, in the main, the old wagon road constructed under the direction of Lieut. Napier, now Lord Napier, of Magdala. This road has been in existence for many years, and was the earliest made for reaching this much-needed sanitarium, which was established as early as 1840. As the mountains rise almost directly from the plain, a rapid ascent is noticeable from the first, and we had been but a mile or two on our way when sharp curves became frequent—in some instances not exceeding a radius of 75 feet. The forest-trees also increased in number, and at some points we passed thick jungles of enormous bamboo and cane, and as we turned the sharp projecting points of the mountain, beautiful views of the valleys and plains beyond presented themselves. At 2,000 feet we met the tea plantations, which became an object of interest. The plant itself does not, in this section, exceed three feet in height, and resembles the gooseberry bush as much as anything I now think of. Fortunately I met on the train Mr. Henry Wathen, manager of the " Springside Tea Gardens," who gave me a great deal of interesting and valuable information respecting the culture of tea. I was surprised to learn from him that the best Darjeeling tea commanded the highest price in London market of any in the world. You lovers of good tea may as well make a note of that. The amount sent out is not great—about 10,000,000 pounds The entire India product is about 60,000,000 pounds. The tea is grown at all available points along the side of the mountains up to this point, and in very many instances the land is terraced in order to sustain the plant and prevent the rains from washing it away. Tea requires considerable moisture, combined with heat. From 140 to 150 inches of rainfall gives the requisite amount. So far as I could learn, the only difference between green and black tea lies in the curing—the former being subject to longer and greater heat than black tea. Both teas are picked from the same plants, and the young and tender leaves give the best article. As tea can be grown in the plain below, and the yield is greater per acre, I naturally asked why the mountains were chosen. The reply was that the mountain tea was stronger and of a finer flavor—hence it is much used in mixing with other teas. The yield in the plain country is about 540 pounds per acre, while up here it varies 240 to 320 pounds.

We reached this comfortable hotel at 4 P. M., and were cordially greeted by our hostess, Mrs. Roberts, who at once directed fires to be built in our rooms and offered us a refreshing cup of tea. During the last part of the journey a fog had settled about us, and every one was anxious to learn the prospects of seeing the snowy range at sunset or in the early morning. Mrs. Roberts was positive that we would have that pleasure, as all indications pointed that way ; and just before the sun went down we caught a glimpse of Kinchinjunga and some of its neighboring peaks. I ordered a pony to be ready at 7 o'clock the following morning, that I might make the excursion to Senchal, six miles away, from which the peak of Mount Everest is visible. I was roused at 6 A. M., and was out on the terrace just as the sun was tinging the topmost peaks of the snowy range—

prominent among which is " Old Kinchan," as he is called for short. The morning was beautifully clear and the whole range, although 5o miles away, seemed only a short distance off,

Securing a cup of coffee and a couple of soft boiled eggs, I was soon away on the active mountain pony that had been ordered for me. The rise is continuous almost the entire journey, and you have some superb views of Darjeeling, the Snowy Mountains and the various valleys of the Himalyas. The ride takes you through the Military Sanitarium of Jalapah and one or two mountain villages, where you meet the hardy, strongly-built mountain man—an entirely different type from the resident of the plain. The mountain-eers show most distinctly the Tartar peculiarities of feature—broad faces, the almond eye of the Chinese, etc., and some even wore " pig tails "—showing their connection with that race. Along the mountain road I met numerous parties of wood-carriers, who were on their way to the Darjeeling market with a back-load of wood. Their burdens would have crushed the ordinary Calcutta native. They all greeted me cordially, and there was an air of independence about them that called for attention. Many of their women were exceedingly fair, and in some faces the rich blush of the European was visible.

I reached Senchal at 8 A. M., where the pocket aneroid marked 8,45o feet, and a little more climbing brought me to Tiger Hill, 8,8oo feet. From this.

DARJEELING. HIMALAYA'S IN THE DISTANCE. INDIA.

elevation the view of the entire range was complete, and included Mount Everest (over 100 miles away) and its two adjoining peaks. Like the one from the top of Rhigi, in Switzerland, it is very comprehensive, and is most satisfactory. You may naturally ask which I prefer, and I'm compelled to say the Swiss one, as the latter combines more beauties, such as lake and river scenery. The volume of snow, too, in the Himalayas is much less—owing no doubt, to its lower latitude.

I returned to the hotel in time for a late breakfast, and at 11 A. M. shall be off for Calcutta. I would like to remain longer in this grand place, but when one is making a tour of the world an eye must be had to the countries beyond, and which should be reached at the proper season—particularly Japan, which all travelers unite in 'pronouncing one of the most attractive and interesting that they meet with in the course of this 25,000 miles trip. I find up here several agreeable and interesting English people—all, like myself, visiting it for a view of the snowy range, and to make a journey over the Darjeeling and Himalaya Railway—one of the most remarkable in English territory.

I observe on the books of this hotel the names of quite a number of our countrymen, some of whom I've met before in my journey; but some are evidently bound to the westward, and have come from Japan, China and elsewhere. As the dates of all

are quite recent, this may reasonably be regarded as
a sort of half-way house in the journey round the
world.

XV.

CALCUTTA TO MADRAS.

AUSTRIO-HUNGARIAN STEAMER "ARGO",
MOUTH OF HOOGLY RIVER, INDIA, TEMP. IN SHADE, 82°.
February 14th, 1886.

FROM the caption of this you will see that I am leaving India, where I've passed nearly two months most agreeably and, I trust, profitably. My last impressions are certainly delightful, as at Calcutta I fell into most hospitable hands, and the last week was passed at the cozy home of Mr. and Mrs. J. Go——n—he a member of the Bengal Bank. I made their acquaintance on the way from Brindisi to Bombay, and on reaching Calcutta (on my return from Darjeeling) they insisted upon my coming to their house—a change I was glad to accept, as India hotels are not over attractive, and those of Calcutta seemed to be placed in the midst of the "smelliest" district of the city.

Government House is near the same locality, and

I wonder how the Viceroy can stand the foul smells that I noticed when passing in front of his residence. Perhaps this accounts for his passing such a small portion of the time in the city, as he goes every week to a country place near town, and in the hot weather to Simla, a hill station up in the Punjab, some 1,200 miles from Calcutta. I would not have you think Government House an unattractive one, as everything is done to render it a desirable residence. It is in the midst of a large " compound "—containing, I should judge, some seven acres—which is shut off from the streets that surround it by dense tropical foliage, conspicuous among which is the bamboo. The structure itself is large and in the classical style of architecture—the main building having a circular portico supported by Ionic columns. The wings are connected with the main building by semi-circular galleries. The grounds are well kept and numerous plants are distributed through them. One or two pieces of ordnance have conspicuous positions at both the north and south fronts. The state rooms of the interior are very large and imposing ; the throne-room is especially so. Numerous portraits of former Governor-Generals (as they were originally styled) adorn its walls, as also those of the dining and ball rooms.

The entire house was thrown open on the night of February 1st, when a grand ball was given in honor of the foreign officers. It was a large assemblage,

principally, made up from the military, and the number of gaudy uniforms, added to the rich toilets of the
ladies, made it a gay affair. The Viceroy wore a
rich uniform, and Lady Dufferin was handsomely
dressed in dark velvet and wore a species of crown,
or tiara, of precious stones upon her head. Dancing
was kept up 'till a late hour; but, as I had attended
rather a large dinner party before going, I did not
feel disposed to remain late—hence must be excused
from telling who were the belles of the evening.

The Viceroy rarely goes out unattended, and a
large troop of native lancers forms his body guard.
They are picked men, mounted upon large English
horses, and their rich uniform and fine appearance
usually attract attention. It is probably good policy
to have the Viceroy thus escorted, as the native mind
is impressed by such stately show. On the other
hand, without an escort, their estimate of him would
probably be lessened.

Calcutta has long borne the reputation of being a
city of palaces. I don't know that it fully maintains
this title, but certainly the old merchant princes of
Calcutta built handsome residences, the principal
portion of which are located on Chowringee Road
and face a large open mall, where most of the sports
are held by the Europeans. It is a pretty feature
of the city, and is nicely kept. Most of the driving is
done, in the afternoons, along roads that border it.
The club houses are also fine buildings and many are

located on Chowringee Road. Prominent among
these are the Bengal and the United Service, the
former at one time the residence of Mr. T. B.
Macaulay afterwards Lord Macaulay; it was founded
in 1827. In case of temporary residence in the city
it is well to become a member. You pay a small
sum as an initiation fee, and after that only for your
room and such refreshments as you may order.
Many travelers having friends among the members,
and only passing a few days, prefer paying the initiation fee, as one is made so much more comfortable than at a hotel. Mr. Pa——n, manager of the
French Bank kindly offered to put me up, but added:
"As you are to stop at a private house, I don't think
anything will be gained." Hence I did not seek an
election. One of the most interesting excursions that
I made was to the Botanical Gardens, which are
down the river (on the right bank) and some three
miles from the city. The collection of plants and rare
trees is most extensive, and the managers have the
reputation of having distributed more plants than
any other garden in the world. The gardens cover
some 270 acres and near the centre is the famous
Banyan tree (*Ficus indica*), the arms of which cover
ground 800 feet in circumference. Immediately
opposite these gardens and on the Calcutta side of
the river, is the residence of the King Oudh and his
numerous retainers. He is kept under surveillance
and amuses himself after his pleasure. One of his

hobbies is the collection of animals and birds. I saw swarms of pigeons flying about the various buildings, and it was stated he had 50,000—many of choice varieties. I did not visit his palace, being rather "used up" with a cold and fatigued by sight seeing elsewhere.

Old Fort William, completed in 1773 under Lord Clive, is an interesting work and a very strong one for its day; it is on the side of the Esplanade nearest the river, and but a short distance from it. Its plan is sort of an irregular octagon, with five sides looking landward and three on the river; it is surrounded by a ditch 30 feet deep and 50 broad, can mount 600 guns, and hold a garrison of 10,000 men.

Coming from the upper country, one is rather struck with the absence of the turban among the natives —a feature that did not impress me pleasantly, as it is always picturesque and to my taste adds greatly to the appearance of the average native ; but it is a fact that a great many go entirely bare-headed, and I noticed this the case with the merchant and legal class (or, at least, I took them as such); on the river and among the boatmen the practice of going without any head covering is almost general.

I should be glad if I could describe the ordinary river boat, for it is a most picturesque affair, with its stern elevated high above the rowers, who occupy the bow, or forward part ; but I hardly think myself up to making it plain to your readers. I am sure the average South Side bayman would be amused if he could see one of these native crafts.

I bade good-bye to my friends in the city late in the afternoon of the 11th—preferring to come on board the day before, as the ship was advertised to sail early on the morning of the 12th. "Rama" my servant, accompanied me to the steamer, and really seemed to regret parting. He was profuse in his gratitude for what I had done for him, and especially gratified that I had given him the opportunity of visiting so many of the places sacred to his Hindoo gods. I know that he spent his money freely among the Hindoo priests at Benares, and I believe he had to pay well at other points, so that when settling with him I gave quite a liberal sum as "backshish." His eyes brightened up and he made several demonstrations of gratefulness. Well, he was in the main a good servant and, I believe, honest and faithful, and I trust my certificate of character will soon secure him another place. I know that those who have employed Portuguese servants, who are usually Christians, often complain that they were lazy and, when they got a chance, would drink up their master's liquor. "Rama" never drank anything intoxicating as it is against the Hindoo creed, and was never absent except by permission.

While on the subject of servants I will state that in course of conversation, my hostess at Calcutta told me it required sixteen men servants for her

rather quiet establishment, and their average pay
per month was something more than $4 each, with
which sum they supported themselves entirely. She
also said that when they kept their own horses three
additional men would be necessary. At the present
time they were using a livery stable horse and
coupe, for which they paid about $50 per month.
All these items sound absurdly cheap to us, but under the caste system only certain men can perform
certain styles of work, and hence the necessity for
so large a force. Three or four good servants, with
us, would really accomplish more than the entire 19
Indian natives—their methods of doing everything
being so crude that no attempt is made to save
labor, and where population is so dense as in India,
it might be fatal to the masses if the labor of a few
could be made to accomplish as much as is now performed by the many. The average daily compen-
sation for agricultural labor is from two to four
" anas " per day—that is, from 6 to 12 cents, of our
money—on which they subsist themselves.

I had ample time, while lying in the river, to observe the shipping, most of which was anchored to
buoys. Very few vessels were alongside of piers.
In truth, the rise and fall of tide (from 10 to 15 feet)
does not easily admit of piers, I believe only the
P. & O. and the British India Lines have accommodations of this description. There are some points
where other steamers receive and discharge their

freight, but they are only permitted to occupy such places for a short time. The navigation of the Hoogly is exceedingly difficult, and is attended with many dangers. Most captains have a great dread of it, and they have reason for their fears, as, owing to shifting sands, vessels grounding are liable to turn over in a few moments, and there are many instances given of loss from this cause. Fortunately they have a superior class of pilots, and this inspires confidence. Owing to river regulations (all no doubt most wise and necessary), sand bars, etc., we were from 8 A. M. on the 12th, to 1 P. M. on the 13th making a distance of about 90 miles, and this in a steamer drawing little more than 18 feet of water. This will give your seafaring readers an idea of the difficulties of navigating the Hoogly—which, by the by, in many features resembles the Mississippi, particularly on its left bank, which has a levee along a portion of the distance. The crooks and turns in the river, sand bars, etc., all tend to remind one of America's great stream, but the vegetation of this is more of a tropical character, and the date and other varieties of the palm tree form the chief foliage along its banks.

This letter is probably the last you will get from India, and your readers may naturally ask the question: " Will a trip to India pay?" I answer: "Most emphatically, *Yes.*" The interest in the journey has never for a moment flagged, and it undoubtedly would have been far greater had I prepared myself more thoroughly for the journey. My appreciation would have been keener, and less time would have been consumed in looking up the chief objects of interest, had I known exactly what they were and where they were to be found. Let those who have the time and inclination, and sufficient zest for travel not to care for a few discomforts, come and see for themselves. A first class return ticket by the best steamers will not cost much more than a winter passed in Florida, and I am confident that the variety and change of scene will be tenfold greater and more diverting.

Our steamer touches for a few hours at Madras, where I mail this, and then proceeds direct to Colombo, in Ceylon, where I shall be detained some four or five days for a P. & O. steamer to take me to Penang, Singapore and Hong Kong. As I do not propose making any longer stay at those points than a through steamer usually does, you may not hear from me more than once until reaching Hong Kong, about March 15th.

I enclose with this some leaves of the tea plant, which I intended to send in a letter from Darjeeling They will be thoroughly dried up and may be crumbled before reaching Long Island, but you may be able to form some idea of the leaf, which in its prepared state furnishes the beverage that stimulates without intoxicating.

XVI.

MADRAS TO CEYLON.

AUSTRIO-HUNGARIAN STEAMER "ARGO",
NEARING COLOMBO, ÇEYLON.
TEMP. IN SHADE, 80°.
February 19th, 1886.

OUR stay in Madras was longer than anticipated (being some twenty-two hours), which gave us a good opportunity of seeing the city. Approaching Madras from the sea, you get a fine view of its public buildings, several of which are located immediately upon the shore, leaving only a wide drive and traffic-way between them and the water. The post office is the most prominent, and presents a good appearance, with its conspicuous towers, visible a long way up and down the coast. None of the other public buildings are especially noticeable.

Driving through the city does not greatly impress one with either its beauty or attractiveness, but some of the roads in the European quarter are beautifully lined with trees and furnish fine drives. Mount Road, which leads to a mount some eight miles away, is one of the most prominent, and I saw some fine equipages in the course of the hour I was on it. A drive along the Beach Road, in the direction of Fort St. George, is another favorite resort and gives one a refreshing breeze from the sea—most acceptable, I should judge, as Madras seems to have the reputation of being an intensely hot place. When I visited the office of the agent of this line and remarked that he kept the "punka" going, his reply was: "Yes, and it's necessary all the year round."

The harbor of Madras is entirely artificial, and owes every safety it posseses to its breakwater, constructed originally in the form of the letter "U," with an opening in its base towards the sea. This portion was materially damaged during a cyclone of three or four years since. Nearly all steamers receive and discharge their cargoes from lighters, and during the stormy season the natives use a species of high-sided surf boat, without knees or braces, and the planks which lap each other, are sewed instead of being nailed together—their keel, stern and bow pieces being the only substantial parts. I was told the planks were exceeding light and porous, and many are cut from the palm tree. They swim very high and, having large crews can be run well up on the beach on landing. (See representation on cover of book.)

The fishing boat, large numbers of which we passed some distance at sea and on entering and leaving the harbor, is an odd-looking affair (a species of

catamaran), made up of three or four logs bound together, which are brought to a point in front so as to
form a species of bow.   They were usually occupied
by a couple of natives, who were entirely nude
except a strip of cotton cloth about their loins and an
odd-shaped, comical straw hat.   The hot sun has no
terrors for them, and their black bodies actually glist-
ened under its fierce rays.   Some varieties of the
fish taken are excellent and firm in flesh, as I can
testify from those we had the following morning for
breakfast.

Nothing of material interest has occurred upon
this voyage from Calcutta.   The sea has been, for
most of the way, as calm as the poorest sailor could
desire. I've passed a good share of the time on deck,
under the double canvas awning, and often sleeping
there in preference to the cabin.   Our rate of speed
averaged about 9 knots per hour, and the distance,
some 1,380 miles, has consumed—owing to various
detentions already alluded to —about eight days.   I
shan't be sorry to have a few days on shore before
embarking on another sea trip.   The table fare has
been in the main good, and the dishes (largely made
up of ragouts) have been nicely served—a pleasant
change from much of the Calcutta and India cooking;
but I shall be glad to get back to English tastes and
modes, which I'm likely to find on the P. & O. steamer, and which I take from Colombo to Hong Kong

I was not very pleasantly impressed with the

Madras native. All are exceedingly dark. Their skins are about the color of that of the African, and the type of feature far less attractive than that met with in the northern section of India. I feel quite confident that the most interesting portion of this country—at least to the average traveler—is the Northwestern Provinces. As I shall complete this letter after reaching Colombo, I close for the present.

Grand Hotel, Nuwara Eliya, Ceylon, February 23*d,* *1886.*—We reached Colombo early on the 20th, and had a fine view of the harbor and the town, which is built along the water. The native houses are low and unattractive in appearance, but some of the Government buildings are substantially built, and are quite imposing. The Grand Oriental Hotel, where I passed one night, is one of the cleanest and very best met with in the East, but the night was too hot for sleeping with any comfort, and I was not sorry after a visit to the banker's, and a short drive through the town, to take the train for this point, which is in the interior of the island, and some 150 miles from Colombo. It has been for many years a sanitarium for the residents of that city, who are only too glad to escape the hottest months—March, April and May—by resorting to this elevated region, some 6,200 feet above the sea. I am here a little in advance, as you see, of the fashionable season ; still I'm very glad to be here and breathe an atmosphere which has some real ozone in it.

Of the ride here I can't speak in too high terms, as it impressed me as one of the very finest, for a railway journey, that I've taken. For the first twenty-five miles out from Colombo the line of road passes through a flat country, much of which is devoted to the cultivation of rice, and we saw that grain in various stages ; the larger portion had, however, been gathered. At·Ambepussa—or even below it—we entered the mountains, when the scenery becomes grand. The line skirts along bold mountain precipices, furnishing superb views of valleys and mountain streams, the beauty of which is heightened by rich tropical foliage, and some of the grandest-colored flowers I've ever seen. There is such a rapid succession of these beautiful views that one is kept constantly on the alert if he does not care to miss any, and I certainly was on the look out for most of them. At Peredeniya the road branches—one going to Kandy, where there is a very comfortable hotel and quite a resort (as it's some 3,000 feet or more above the sea.) The main line, however, continues on in a south-easterly course. and soon enters the great tea- and coffee-growing districts of the island. The ascent is not, perhaps, so rapid as before ; still, the rise is continuous, and as the train passes from one ridge to another. or turns the sharp projecting bluff, some beautiful views of the mountain streams and valleys present themselves. We are now in the midst of the largest tea plantations, or estates, as they are variously styled. A few years since, only coffee was grown, but a blight (I believe a species of rust) attacked the plant and the coffee grower's prospects were ruined. Fortunately he tried the tea plant, and its success has been so great that he now talks boldly of driving the India tea from the English market. However true this may prove, I believe the quotation of Ceylon tea in the London market does in some degree warrant the high stand the present planter claims for it, and the crop (now some 8,000,-000 of pounds) it is estimated will exceed 12,000,000 pounds in the course of the next two years.

Nearly the entire labor employed in the tea and coffee culture is imported from Southern India, and is largely from a class, or tribe, called Tamals, the average Ceylonese holding himself above this class of work. Still, they are agriculturists, and grow most of the rice that is produced in Ceylon, and it is possible that in time they may fall into line. This method of importing labor has been going on some thirty years or more. The planters tell me that wages are higher in Ceylon than in India—the rate here being from four to six *anas* (12 to 18 cents) per day, while in India it is 6 to 12 cents—in each case the laborer finding himself.

Nearly all the first-class travelers on the train were tea planters or friends recently from England, who had come out to Ceylon to pass a few weeks. At Hatton we left a number, and at Kotagala station a party of eight ladies and gentlemen left the train, bound for the hospitable bungalow of some successful tea planter; so that when the train arrived at Nanuoya, the terminus of the line, there was left only some five or six travelers (or "globe trotters" as some times designated,) bound for this point, distant about four and one-half miles, and made by coach in something less than an hour.

We are very comfortable at this house, managed by a European, but owing to rain we have been kept indoors. However, as there is not a very great deal to be seen, the deprivation is not great; but in fine weather there are some pretty drives, and for the Alpine climber some peaks that will test the mettle.

There is a choice of hotels in this place—the Criterion being almost next door—but as this is better filled, and as Prince Napoleon (son of Prince Jerome Napoleon) and his companions are to arrive this evening, I presume we may flatter ourselves that we are at the best one.

The above is rather a rough description of a trip to the mountains of Ceylon, but let me urge upon any of your readers who contemplate a visit to this Island not to leave this journey out, as it more than pays; besides it may save the necessity of a trip to Java; at least, I propose making it answer.

I have not encountered any ferocious animals in the course of this trip to the mountains, but during a visit made this afternoon to the botanical gardens, which are some six miles from this place, the man-ager conducted us to a tank, about which we saw abundant evidence of there having been quite a large band of wild elephants, and as this is likely to be as near as I shall come to shooting one of those enormous beasts, I make the most of what I saw. They are very fond of the tree fern, and had they come a little nearer his bungalow might have gotten into the fernery, and played sad havoc with one of the choicest and most attractive parts of the garden.

I return to Colombo by train to-morrow, and the following day take passage in the P. & O. steamer "Hydaspes," for Penang, Singapore and Hong Kong —the only stops being about a day each at the two ports first named—and I shall continue in this vessel to her destination—a trip of over 3,000 miles.

I've neglected mentioning the native Cyngolese— an omission I wish to amend by saying I find him very similar, in feature and manners, to the Indian of the North—his dress differing in some essential features, but especially in the absence of the turban for which he substitutes a comb, precisely the same as is often worn by young girls, with us to keep the hair from their eyes. His wife, on the other hand, never wears any, but in place uses a large pointed hair pin, usually highly ornamental. Both sexes "do up" the back hair after the Grecian style, and its often puzzling to discover the sex when the comb does not happen to be visible.

I observe in Ceylon the same propensity or pas-sion, on the part of the women, for jewelry as pre-vails in India, and enormous rings for the nostrils and ears are worn. In some instances the ear is pierced in half a dozen places. In addition to these she wears rings on her toes and fingers, and anklets and bracelets. Even the men display a passion for finger rings, and some financiers say it would be im-possible to make gold a standard medium in India, as it would be melted up as soon as issued the mass of the population not understanding the use-fulness of placing it in a savings institution or in some solid investment.

In the first portion of this letter I've spoken of the Madras fishing boat as an odd affair ; and not easily described ; but the Ceylonese one is still more odd, and defies my powers of giving any correct idea of it. I thought over it for a time, and finally settled the question by purchasing a model of one, and if I can manage to put it together again (for it was too cumbersome to pack up in full rig,) I shall be able to give my friends a correct impression of it without taxing my descriptive powers.

I enclose some flowers of the coffee plant, gather-ed at the terminus of the line of rail; the flower of this plant is pure white, with a decidedly strong per-fume, and resembles the orange blossom as much as anything I now think of.

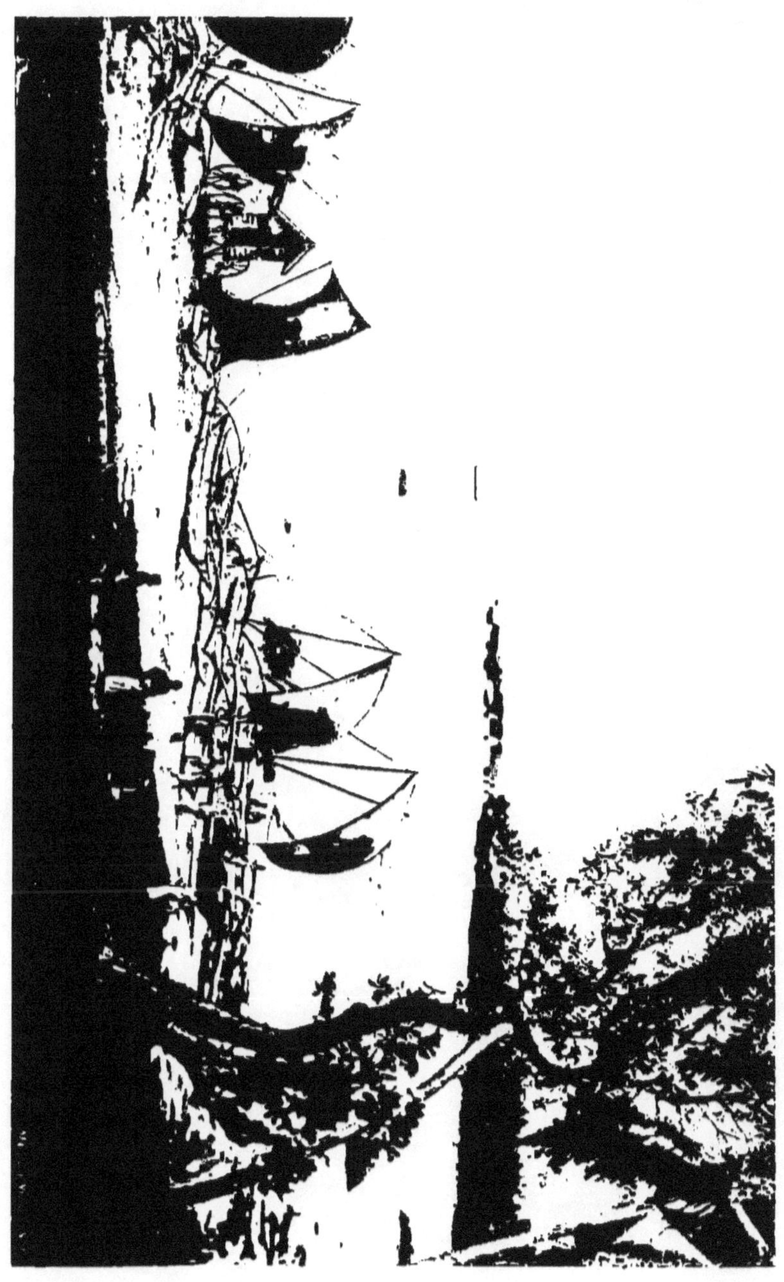

XVII.

CEYLON TO HONG KONG.

STMR. "HYDASPES," STRAITS OF MALACCA, NEARING PENANG,
ABOUT LAT. 5.35 N., LONG., 95.58 E.,
March 1st, 1886.

ALTHOUGH my stay in Colombo was short, by making good use of the time I managed to accomplish considerable, and visited many of the places of interest, a description of which was given in my last. I omitted, however, to speak of a pleasant afternoon's excursion to Mount Lavinia, which I made in company with Mr. H. H. Sparkes, of Bangalore, a fellow passenger from Madras to Colombo on the steamer Argo. Mount Lavinia is a small eminence on the coast, some ten miles south of Colombo, and is reached by rail. It was formerly the residence of Sir E. Barnes, one of the Governors of Colombo, and the marine villa built by him is now the Grand Hotel. The point on which it is located is open to the sea on three sides. and it is rare that one does not get a refreshing breeze. As we had planned to take a late lunch, or "tiffin," there, our appetites were none the less keen from the long wait, and also from the tempting dishes that were supplied. The whitebait was cooked to perfection, and the tender-loin steak was the best I've found in India. All was washed down with a bottle of excellent Rhenish wine.

On our way to and from Mount Lavinia we passsd many of the bungalows, of the European residents, which are prettily placed in groves of cocoanut palms, with their fronts directly on the sea. Many are of modern styles, but all are arranged with refer-ence to catching every breath of air coming from the water, as Colombo is very hot and one requires all the air that is stirring. The line of rail also passes near the Galle-Face-Esplanade and Club House, where we saw a large assemblage of Europeans and natives indulging in various sports, such as polo, pony racing, tennis, cricket and golf. It certainly is most creditable to the English residents that they keep alive these many exercises, as one would hardly look for them in a place where the heat is so excessive; but they usually practice just at sunset, when the direct rays of the sun have lost much of their power. The sports are most healthful and prevent the liver from becoming torpid—one of the consequences of inactivity in hot climates.

The Colombo Club is one of the pleasant resorts of the island, and thanks to Mr. A. Forsyth, of the firm of Delmege, Reed & Co., I was given not only an excellent dinner, but also enjoyed the privileges of the Club during my stay; a compliment I fully appreciated, as the club house is so constructed, and so placed with reference to the sea, that if there is a cool spot on the island it is apt to be found there, and I think my friends on Long Island owe to the comfort there, as, also, the facilities furnished for letter writing, some of the missives dispatched to them.

I had in Colombo my first experience in a jinricki-shaw, a species of perambulator, or baby carriage of large growth.

The Coolie who draws you, lowers the shafts and you take your seat, when he steps between them and, raising them to the height of his waist, trots off with his load. This two-wheeled vehicle is provided with a top, is hung on light springs, and is very comfortable indeed. I timed the Coolie that brought me from the Club to the Grand Oriental Hotel, distance, about one mile—and he was some fifteen minutes making the trip. As I'm likely to use this species of carriage very extensively in my travels in China and Japan, it occurred to me that some description might be of interest.

We left the pretty harbor of Colombo, on the afternoon of February 25th, and have been since making good progress toward Penang—the ship averaging some 260 miles per day—about as good speed as most of them make. She is of the old type of steamers, with flush deck, but I find her very comfortable indeed. My cabin is on the port side—a point to be remembered in making the passage to the Eastward—and by the aid of a species of wind-sail in the large square port a constant current of air is passing directly over me, making it possible to write with the thermometer marking 85 degrees and over. We passed, this morning, shortly after breakfast, Acheen, the most northerly point of the Island of Sumatra. The land is very bold, and it makes a most excellent point of departure for Penang—lying almost due east.

We have an unusually large number of first cabin passengers—about fifty. Some of these, like myself, are making the grand *tour du Monde*. Several of them I've met before in my travels in India, and it's very agreeable comparing notes on the country passed over, or scenes that each have encountered ; but the larger share are temporary residents of the Straits, Settlements, China, etc., returning from a good long vacation in England to resume their various duties. All the various houses of the East seem to encourage their employees by giving them liberal leaves of absence without reduction of pay— I think one year out of every five. It seems to insure a heartier interest in their work, besides rendering the individual more vigorous and better able to resist the debilitating effects of this hot climate.

I stop writing for the present, but will resume again after leaving Penang, where we are due some time to-morrow afternoon.

P. & O. Steamer "Hydaspes," March 3rd, 1886.— The approach to the harbor of Penang was an agreeable one, as we skirted along the shores of Penang Island for many miles. High hills, almost mountains, come directly down to the water's edge—heavily wooded, save where the farmer or planter has made a clearing. As we approached the anchorage we passed numerous fish wiers, made by planting stakes in a square form. I did not learn the method of getting said fish into these inclosures, but presume there is one. We anchored about 4 P. M. on the 2d, and, finding there would be a delay of five hours, a party of us started for the shore in one of the native boats, called sampan—a triangular-shapd affair. The stern is broader than the bow, and the former terminates in a couple of pointed and upward curved gunwales—the rower standing and facing the bow.

As soon as possible after landing we secured a carriage, as the sun was still hot, and made a tour of the town. We also drove some four miles into the country, to a pretty garden and water-fall. We passed on the way several carriages and dog carts driven by Chinamen—all stylish—and one of the finest bungalows we passed proved to be the residence of a wealthy Chinese. In truth, "John Chinaman" is fast driving out the original proprietors of this land—the Malays. Leaving Penang at 11 P. M. on the 2d, we continued our course down the Straits of Malacca towards Singapore, which is about Latitude 1.20° N.—at least so my map says, this will be the lowest point reached. After leaving there our course will be northward and toward cooler latitudes.

One of the noticeable features of these very low latitudes is the position of some of the heavenly bodies—as, for instance, the north star, so prominent in our country, is here so near the horizon that it is hardly visible to the naked eye—much below 5 degrees. The Southern Cross, a well-defined collection of stars, in the Southern Hemisphere, although not an early riser, is very conspicuous when once up, and the arrangement of its four, bright stars forms an admirable Roman crucifix ; but the Great Bear still retains its prominence in the heavens, and I don't think anyone from our clime feels like exchanging it for the Southern beauty. Its " pointers " are still as true to their work and indicate as accurately the position of the Pole Star, in spite of the fact that the light from it—owing to the density of the medium near the horizon —fails to reach us.

The straits have been exceedingly warm—the thermometer often marking from 87 to 90 degrees and with but little breeze. I observed from the color of the water that we were on soundings, and questioning our captain concerning it, learned that it does not exceed six or seven fathoms for much of the way, and that the channel is a narrow one. He added that in former days, before the coast was so well lighted, vessels were often compelled to anchor at night.

The Strait Settlements, of which Penang, Malacca and Singapore are the principal towns, are all under a Colonial Governor (English), who resides at Singapore, and since the threatened Russian war of last year, liberal provision has been made for the fortification of its most important harbor, Singapore, where extensive earth-works have been constructed. We reach that port early to-morrow, and, as we take on quite a large supply of coal, some time will be necessary, thus enabling us to have a good look at that rather extensive and important port—one of the most so, in fact, in the route to the far East.

I leave off for the present, and will continue this after sailing from Singapore.

At Sea, March 7th, 1886.—We entered the harbor of Singapore on the morning of the 4th—a very snug one indeed—and where the P. & O. and other steam lines have their piers—most convenient—as the water is of sufficient depth to permit ships lying alongside wharves, as with us—one of the very few instances met with in the course of this journey.

"Ship sails at 5 P.M.," was the announcement on
the bulletin board of our steamer shortly after she
had been laid alongside her wharf, so that all who
had the intention of visiting the city were soon seeking a carriage to take them—the distance being
some four miles. I looked over the carriage stand
and picked out what I thought the most active of
the ponies, for none were animals more than ten
or twelve hands high. The one I selected was not
a beauty, and was rather thin in flesh ; but as I had
some six hours' work out of him, I can testify
to the fact that he was "a good one."

Nearly all these animals are brought from the
mountain districts of Sumatra—a section of it called
Deli furnishing the principal portion. The driver
seemed to sympathize with my impatience to reach
the city, and kept his pony at a good pace. We
were soon at the business office of Behn, Meyr &
Co.—passing on the way lots of other vehicles,
among which were numerous jin-ricki-shaws. I was
very kindly received by one of the members of the
firm, and after transacting my little business affair
was urged to return at 1 o'clock and lunch with him
at the Singapore Club, which invitation I accepted.
I then drove to the office of our Consul, Major
Studor, who gave me the latest information from our
country and also a supply of New York papers—the
only ones I had seen since leaving Venice, on December 3d, last. The Major has been for many years

our representative at this city, and I learned, was very popular. The lunch at the Club proved to be a good one, and was a most agreeable change from ship fare. " Ye heathen Chinee," in a white dress and with a long pig-tail waited upon us and did his work well. My host stated " that he was a good waiter, but required watching."

The Club House is one of the finest buildings of the city, and its location, directly facing the harbor, insures a breeze at almost all hours.

I was fortunate in finding at Singapore a number of letters from home friends, for which I wish here to acknowledge my thanks.

On leaving Singapore we had a superb view of its harbor and the surrounding hills, which serve as an admirable setting for the lower town. Conspicuous among its tropical vegetation is the so-called "traveler's palm," the leaves of which shoot out, at a considerable height. from a central stalk in a fan-like form, and are most graceful. It derives its name from the fact that the weary traveler can, by cutting an incision in its bark, draw from the tree a cup of cool and refreshing water.

Some hours after leaving Singapore we passed the meridian of 105 degrees and 57 minutes East Longitude, and as New York City is 74 degrees and 3 minutes West, it placed us as near as practicable 180 degrees from that point, or half way around the world. As it may interest you to learn the distance traveled in order to reach this prominent position, I append a list of the various journeys:

	Miles.
From New York City to Queenstown by sea	2,601
From Queenstown to Liverpool by sea	221
From Liverpool to London by land, about	180
From London to Paris, by land and water, about	220
From Paris to Venice by land, about	720
From Venice to Brindisi, by water, about	395
From Brindisi to Alexandria, by water, about	825
From Alexandria to Suez, by rail, about	220
From Suez to Aden, by water, about	1,308
From Aden to Bombay, by water, about	1,664
From Bombay to Lahore, via Jeypore and Delhi, by rail, about	1,300
From Lahore to Calcutta, via Allahabad and Benares, by rail, about	1,300
From Calcutta to Madras, by water, about	770
From Madras to Colombo, by water, about	610
From Colombo to Penang, by water, about	1,278
From Penang to Singapore, by water, about	381
	13,993

And, adding to these the distance likely to be made in further journeys to the Eastward, viz:

	Miles.
From Singapore to Hong Kong, by water, about	1,437
From Hong Kong to Shanghai, by water, about	870
From Shanghai to Nagasaki, by water, about	500
From Nagasaki to Yokohama, by water, about	735
From Yokohama to San Francisco, by water, about	4,500
From San Francisco to New York, by rail, about	3,300
	11,342
Or, total of distances traveled in a tour around the world—starting from New York City and going Eastward, about	25,335

We are steaming alone finely through the China

Sea, and with every indication that we will be in Hong Kong by the 10th or 11th of March—a haven all will be glad to reach, as fifteen days at sea is no slight test of one's powers of endurance, and during the last days of our voyage we have been subject to rather a strong northeast " Monsoon "—Chinese for "big wind"—which has shaken us up considerably, and placed our amiability to no slight test.

XVIII.

HONG KONG, CANTON AND MACAO.

HONG KONG HOTEL, HONG KONG, CHINA,
TEMP. BETWEEN 65° AND 70°.
March 21st, 1886.

AS predicted in my last, land was sighted very early on the morning of the 10th, but it was somewhat obscured by a fog, which frequently prevails along the coast during this month.   However, by dint of persevering, our captain managed to "get hold" of one of the numerous islands which lie to the south and west of this, and which he recognized in the fog.   Skirting along it, we came upon the Island of Hong Kong, which should be written (or, rather is called by the Chinese) " Heung Kong," signifying " good harbor." The approach to this city is one the finest I've ever seen.   Bold hills, almost mountains, lie on either shore, and the water is sufficiently deep to permit the larger class of vessels to steam close along them.   The first peep you get of the

CITY AND HARBOR OF HONG KONG.

city, coming from the Southward is of some of its suburban villas, perched high up the mountain sides. Prominent among these is the so-called " Douglas Castle," and near it a Roman Catholic sanitarium, built of light granite, and, from its commanding situation, a very conspicuous object. These prepare one for the more extended view which you get as the steamer makes a sharp turn to the right, when the entire city and its beautiful harbor come in view. The latter seems entirely enclosed save on the side you enter, but a close observation shows that there is a break in the mountain through which vessels departing for the North make their way. When the harbor and city were in full sight, I could not avoid exclaiming : "This is certainly one of the most beautiful and picturesque sights I've ever beheld, and how is it I've never heard more of it?" The water was dotted over with Chinese junks, ships and steamers, and the city, built on terraces, stood out boldly and grandly from the mountain side, and seemed almost to say: "Am I not fair to look upon ?"

We were not permitted to reach the wharf before numerous " sampans " (Chinese boats) were alongside, and runners from various quarters of the city boarded our steamer to secure the Chinese passengers, quite a large number of whom we had brought from Penang and Singapore. The manner in which they handled their boats and boarded us—the steamer running all the while at fair speed—excited both our curiosity and admiration. I frequently, after this, had occasion to use the harbor boats, and found them skilfully handled. Most generally they are in the hands of women, and in some instances I've found a mother, two daughters and a son composing the crew. These families rarely leave the boat, and make it their home.

The pleasant impressions produced on our entering the harbor were not dissipated on landing. The houses are substantially built. The streets of the city are of good width, beautifully kept, and, I should imagine, the drainage very complete. The principal thoroughfare, running parallel with the shores of the harbor, is called Queen's Road, and has some of the finest shops upon it. The Europeans have possession of the part near the hotel, but the Chinese are possesed of equally good buildings but short distances from it, and my experience is that they sell considerably cheaper. It is very evident that the mass of Europeans throughout the East " are not here for their health," but as they usually have but one price for their wares, and stick to these figures—which is not the case with the native dealer—travelers are apt to patronize them when in need of staple articles.

One of the most striking features of the city, to the newly-arrived, is the entire absence of carriages, or the usual vehicles, of cities, but in their place you have a host of jin-ricki-shaws and chairs, the latter a light bamboo affair with a moveable top and easily carried by two men. As the city is built upon the sides of the mountain, much of the travel is up and down hill, and they are in great favor. Nearly every house has one or more, with regularly assigned bearers, who do very little else ; but there are numerous public ones, and whenever you leave the hotel a number rush to secure your patronage, and as the tariff is very light one is tempted to use them frequently. The jin-ricki-shaw is rather better for the level road, as you are taken along at a good pace, and can make some five miles or more per hour.

One of the attractive features of the city is its public gardens, some distance up the sides of the mountain, where one finds beautifully-shaded walks and a rare collection of tropical and northern plants. The present temperature, averaging about 70 degrees, is favorable to the latter, and I find some superb specimens of roses and other valued northern flowers. Flowers are also sold in the streets, and at very low figures. A large basket can be purchased for something more than fifty cents.

Adjoining these gardens are numerous private lawn tennis courts; where both ladies and gentlemen indulge in this healthful game. To the credit of the English be it said, that wherever they establish themselves they are sure to introduce their healthful sports. I attended, a few days since, the meet of the " Hong Kong Amateur Athletic Sports," patronized by the chief officers of the Government, both civil and military, and found the principal merchants, with their assistants, taking part. Prizes were offered for the winners and every inducement held out for the young men to participate, and even the veterans contested in a foot race for a piece of plate. There were all sorts of contests, such as flat and hurdle races, high and long jumps, " putting the shot," and tugs of war, and most of those who took part showed splendid physiques. The attendance was almost general on the part of the Europeans, while a large number of Chinese were also on the ground.

I find here, as I've done in most of their colonies, another excellent English organization, and that is their police, made up of a few Europeans and some Chinese, but mainly of Sikhs from about Delhi and Lahore, India. The latter seem to be entrusted with important posts, and the night service, when they are usually armed with rifles, is largely performed by them. They wear a dark-blue uniform, but retain the red turban of their native country, to which they return, after a certain number of years abroad, with a life pension.

Hong Kong's position renders it an admirable point for excursions in various directions. Manila, Canton, Macao and other places are easily reached—the two latter in less than a day's sail. As Camton is regarded as a typical Chinese city, and rather the least dirty and "smelly," I made my first visit there. A regular line of steamboats ply between this city and Canton. They are modeled after our North River boats. The one we went on is called the "Han Kow," after a large city on the Yangtsze River, and where she formerly ran. We found her exceedingly comfortable—the lower deck being devoted to third-class passengers, the after saloon to seconds, and the first-class occupying the forward saloon. Visiting the lower deck of this steamer, in the course of the journey, I saw as motley a crowd as could well be imagined, most of whom were smoking, and at the same time listening to a professional story teller, who occupied a prominent seat; he had commenced his story as the steamer left the wharf, and it would not end till the boat reached her destination, when he would hand around the hat. I was told that he was a great favorite and drew so well, that the company gave him a free pass, no doubt in the view of increasing the travel by this line.

There were only six of us, and chiefly old companions from the " Hydaspes." Captain Lloyd was exceedingly polite, and pointed out the chief objects of interest along the Canton, or Pearl River, as it now appears on the maps. Chief among these attractions were some islands and the Bogue Forts, which the Chinese have greatly strengthened since or during their trouble with the French. The country along the river is generally flat and devoted to rice culture. At Whompoo, some miles down the river, and near the barrier, we passed the United States war steamer "Marion," Capt. Miller. It was very refreshing to see our flag and feel I was under the protection of American guns. She has since been joined by the "Alert," of lighter draught, which is able to go directly up to the city and lie off that portion of it occupied by Europeans. Our Consul, Mr. Seymour, had asked for this display of force, fearing that the treatment received by the Chinese on the Pacific coast would result in retaliation out here. Perhaps not at present, but when the friends of the murdered and persecuted Chinese begin to return home it is not unreasonable to suppose that their reports may stir up bad feeling, of which the missionaries and a few public officials are liable to be the victims. Still, I wandered through all sections of the city, attended only by a guide—and he a Chinese—and did not meet with any insults, except that I was called a "foreign devil;" but that is a title that Europeans have long since enjoyed, and I believe their friends, the English, are alike so designated; and as a member of the club here told me he had, before knowing me, bet that I was an Englishman, I fancy I could pass muster as one of the Chinaman's friends,

The city of Canton, as you approach it from the river, does not present either an attractive or imposing appearance. Nearly all the houses are low—being of a single story—of a grey color, with no pretentions to architectural effect. The few prominent structures that are striking are the pagodas and the · pawnbrokers' houses, the latter often three stories high, and having peculiar shaped gable-ends. I was told that, in addition to being devoted to the special trade of their owners, they were often patronized as store houses. Being well built and towering high above other buildings, they are not approachable by thieves from the roof, as the average Chinese house is.

Our steamer was not permitted to reach the wharf before she was literally surrounded by a swarm of river boats, seeking the patronage of the Chinese passengers and of the freight. These Canton River boats are a feature of that city, and must number many thousand. The population of them is set down as between two and four hundred thousand, not a member of which own or occupy an acre of ground and who live and bring up families on their small craft. The peculiar shape of some, styled the slipper boat, from their resemblance to the ordinary slipper, is very noticeable. The front portion is covered over and painted, and the rowers propel them from the rear part, and they force them along at high speed.

Having a letter of introduction to Mr. Cunningham, the agent of the house of Russell & Co., in Canton, I was met at the boat by that gentleman, who kindly asked me to his home, and had already secured me a guide for visiting the chief objects of interest in the city; and here I wish to tender my thanks, not only to him, but also to Mr. Huntington, the representative of the house here, who has been as kind as possible—putting me up at the club, dining and giving me letters to their various houses in other parts of China, all of which kindness and attention I fully appreciate.

Having but a limited time to devote to Canton, I had no sooner deposited, my valise at the comfortfortable bungalow of Russell & Co.—for this firm own the residences of their agents in the principal Chinese cities—than I made arrangements with Mac, the guide, for a tour, that afternoon, through the portion of the city nearest our home, and accordingly visited quite a number of shops and a few of the temples, also some of their manufactories. The average Chinese temple is rather a striking structure, and consists of several courts—the high altar or seat of the chief god to which the temple is devoted, being one of the inner buildings. The image, God of War, is a favorite one, being represented by a man of large statue, with long black beard, and with rich Chinese robes. I saw very few worshipers, and I visited temples at various hours, but I did observe a good deal of burning of tapers in jars in front of their images. The practice, too, of burning these tapers in niches at the door of their shops is almost universal, the object of which is, so far as I could gather, to invoke good fortune upon their business affairs. Some Europeans regard this burning of tapers as having a purifying effect upon the atmosphere of Canton, and to a certain degree it disinfects the city. This seems reasonable, and if true, should be encouraged, as its odors are horrible. A most striking architectural feature of these temples is the peculiar and concave form of the ridge, which usually terminates in the figure of a dragon. The eaves are also similarly curved and have dragon ornaments.

Their streets are exceedingly narrow—should not think them over six to eight feet—and their widest thoroughfare, the street of Benevolence and Love, which is in the old town and extends from the east to the west gate, can't be more than twelve feet. Of course, there are no sidewalks, and two good-sized chairs just manage to pass each other. I did all my sight-seeing in a Sedan chair, and the guide claimed a similar luxury.

The pagodas are circular towers of several stories, some reaching nine. They are built of brick and have balconies at each story. I believe the original object of them was for the preservation of some relic of Buddha, but they have since filled the purpose, in Chinese philosophy or religion, of averting evils— at least that is as near their present purpose as I could get at.

My second day's visit in the city was nearly a

repetition of the first, save that I started earlier and saw it after its morning ablutions, and must do it the credit of admitting that there were fewer and less disagreeable smells. I ascended the five-story pagoda, which is at the extreme northern end of the city, and is built upon the wall—for Old Canton is walled in, and its parapets have a number of old iron guns mounted upon them. The view from this pagoda is very extensive and covers the entire city, which presents the same grey, sombre appearance as when approaching it by the river. In this pagoda were several images of heroic size—one, I believe, representing Buddha.

I took some refreshments and then continued my journey, directing my steps towards the Examination Hall—an institution where candidates for political and literary honors are examined every three years. It is capable of holding at one time more than ten thousand persons, who are assigned a species of cell, given a text, and at the end of twenty-four hours are compelled to hand in their treatment of it. Three days are consumed in their examination—a different subject being given each day. Of this large number of candidates something more than 100 are accepted, and they again have to pass a final examination at Pekin, if they wish to attain the highest grades. This is civil service examination of the highest order, but I learn it does not bring about honesty in office, for the reason that the Government itself is not honest, and cares not what the methods of the Mandarins are in collecting taxes, provided the necessary funds reach the capitol. The wonder is how a government so conducted, could have existed for 4,000 years without any material change of form.

After leaving the Examination Hall Mac, the guide, suggested lunch, and took me to what he said was a swell Chinese restaurant. The landlord, Tin-fuk greeted us, on entering, much as Delmonico would, and we were assigned the most select apartment. Mac, who was for 22 years the servant of Archdeacon Gray, of the English Episcopal Church, I naturally inferred knew how to order a dinner, and he did order one—but he did most of the eating, as I could not stand Chinese cooking and did not know how to handle chop sticks. There were no knives and forks, so I contented myself with eating some sweet cakes and taking some refreshing tea. We were offered a beverage, distilled from rice, called *sam-su*, which I found very palatable. At the close of lunch basins of hot water were offered us for washing our hand and faces.

After lunch, I told Mac I wished to visit the court for the examination of criminals, which we did, and after passing through a long line of offices appropriated for lawyers and business matters connected with the court, we entered the apartment where the Judge was trying several cases ; and, I should judge, of various offences. Most of the prisoners were in chains, and on entering to have a hearing, threw themselves on their knees and asked the Judge for mercy, when the examination went on—the object of the Judge being, apparently, to compel the accused to confess or admit the charge against him.   There were three prisoners, who at the same time, were undergoing torture in order to make them confess, as under the Chinese law, capital punishment cannot be inflicted, until the accused admits his crime.   The mode of torture consisted in tying them with their backs to a board, their thumbs and toes brought together behind it, and then pulled as closely as possible—the pain from which must have been excruciating ; but they were not disposed to confess, and I did not care to wait any longer and witness such a scene.

There was no jury, but there appeared to be an attorney who was brow-beating the various prisoners.   Unfortunately a full understanding of the cases was impossible, as Mac's knowledge of English is very limited, and I could not have the entire process explained ; but it seemed to me that Justice in a Chinese court, when one is wrongfully accused, would all depend upon the amouut of money that could be produced to clear the charges.   I've since been told that the cases are all pretty thoroughly investigated by the various subordinates, and a very complete description sent to the Judge previous to trial.   And further, without some compulsory pro-

cess, justice would rarely be reached, as Chinese evidence can be purchased at very low figures.

I also visited some of the prisons, and saw the criminals wearing boards which encircled their necks ; these are some three feet square, are securely fastened on, and have the offences marked on them, one of the prisoners begged me to intercede and get the board removed, as he had not been able to lie down since he was sentenced, but I preferred giving him a small sum, for which he was extremely grateful— These prisons are exceedingly filthy places and I was glad to get away for fear of being covered with vermin. These scenes about tired me of Canton city, and I gladly returned to my comfortable quarters at Mr. Cunningham's. The following morning I took a steamer for Macao, some eighty miles. It is an old Portugese settlement, and, inthe early days of trading with the East, a very prosperous one, as the rich merchants resided there. But its glory has departed, and Hong Kong, from its much finer harbor and greater facilities for business, has robbed it of all its trade, and the port is now almost deserted. The town is prettily situated, and the sea breeze has a fine sweep over it, so that residents of this city often go there for a change.

I have greatly enjoyed my twelve days' stay at this hotel, which, under the management of Mr. Greeley an American, is admirably kept. I believe it ranks first among all hotels in the East. I've also had the pleasure of meeting, at it, Mr. and Mrs. G——e, of West Islip, Suffolk County, Long Island. They are now off on a combined business and pleasure trip to Manila, but are soon to return to their Long Island home.

XIX.

HONG KONG TO SHANGHAI.

STMR. "MELBOURNE," EASTERN SEA, NEARING SHANGHAI,
TEMPERATURE 55°.,
March 25th 1886.

FROM the caption of this you will learn I'm now traveling in a French steamer, my first experience in this long Eastern tour. Three times have I tried the Peninsular and Oriental boats; once the Austrian Lloyds, and now a Messagerie; and I'm bound to admit that I find this ship exceedingly comfortable. The hours of meals are not as congenial to my taste, but the food, combined with the mode of serving, is the best I've yet found, and in point of speed this French boat is much the faster. I also discover that many of the most cosmopolitan class of travelers in this Eastern land give the French line the preference. I've generally chosen the P. & O. boats, as I felt more sure of meeting travelers of similar tastes, as well as speaking my own language, and from the further reason that, in case of accident or break-down, that line has the means and spare vessels to go to your assistance. We have no Chinese passengers—a comfort I duly appreciate. Not only are the decks clear and open from bow to stern, but we escape the horrible smells attending Chinese cooking ; for I believe they indulge in those articles which have to the average Anglo-Saxon the most unsavory odors in the world.

You will notice there has been a material change of temperature, for while in Hong Kong we were in warm summer weather, and wore our lightest clothing. Now, less than two days' travel to the north of it we find winter garments most acceptable, and we go about the decks muffled up in our warmest ulsters. Of course, the suddenness of the change makes a greater impression, and demands much warmer dressing than if we had approached these colder latitudes more gradually.

The prospects are now (if fog does not prevent), that we shall reach Shanghai to-morrow afternoon, and as I do not intend closing this' till I've seen that city and, perhaps, a portion of the great Yangtse river, I leave off writing for the present.

Shanghai Club, Shanghai, China, April 12th 1886.
—Our good ship even exceeded my expectations, and reached the mouth of the Woosung River quite early on the morning of the 26th; but the tide being out

she was not able to cross the bar—hence we were transferred to a tug which brought us to the city. The approach to this town is quite different from that of its rival, Hong-Kong, which, you may recall, is most picturesque. Here the country is flat, and in coming up the river one might fancy himself steaming toward the city of New Orleans, so much does the winding river, muddy water, and general flatness of country resemble the approach to that city,

Shanghai is about 14 miles from the mouth of the Woosung, and the European quarter is the first reached, the native city being further inland. First in order along the river, comes the American Concession, then the English, and after it the French. On the opening of the port this land was set apart by the Chinese Government for the exclusive use of the various powers above mentioned, and the Government of these several colonies is in the hands of their respective representatives. The English system seems to be the prevailing one, and the result is, good broad streets, that are well kept, and good police. The residences are usually large brick structures, stuccoed and built with reference to the heat, which in mid-summer is rather trying.

These residences usually, front on the river, and the warehouses, or " godowns," are in the rear. The system of Concessions above noticed, obtains at nearly all the treaty ports, such as Amoy, Fouchow, Canton, Kiew Kiang, Chinkiang, Hankow and the like, so that in each of the colonies attached to these cities there are most of the conveniences and comforts which pertain to life in Europe or America.

As usual, as you observe from the caption of this, I'm in good luck and enjoying all the comforts of a well-organized club. My room overlooks the river, where most of the shipping is at anchor—the wharfing facilities not being sufficiently extensive to admit of all vessels lying alongside piers. The American flag that floats from the U. S. steamers, Omaha and Marion, is in full view, so that I feel not only comfortable and happy, but also in the land of friends. In truth, it has been my good fortune to feel so at almost every city in the East that I've visited. Armed with a fair amount of letters of introduction, I've never failed to have access to the houses, of the most interesting and intelligent class ; and I've every reason to testify to the hospitality and kindly feelings of all the various nationalities in this far-off land. I'm especially indebted to Mr. C. Vincent Smith, of the American house of Russell & Cor, for kind favors here.

I find here, as I have done in all the other English colonies, that the love of sport has a strong hold upon its residents, and a good race track with the accompanying grand stand and refreshment rooms, has been established in the suburbs of Shanghai. A large share of the business men are out every morning before sunrise, exercising their ponies, a small compact animal brought from the mountain districts of China. A few are tried animals and have a record, but the majority were purchased this season from the traders, and are entirely green and untrained. These last are called *griffins*, and the purchaser has to exercise his best horse knowledge in order to secure even a fair racer. Some amusing scenes occur at these exercises, and there is often an amount of buck-jumping that would compare favorably with that of the wildest Mexican mustang.

As an example of Chinese discipline, which, under the Confucian code exacts the most explicit obedience on the part of children towards the parent, and in case of need the latter can claim a support from their hands. And, as illustrating the extent to which this is carried in China, I will give a most remarkable case of filial devotion on the part of a son towards a widowed and dependent mother. It was told me by a very reliable officer, a member at the time of the staff of General Cameron, commanding English forces in China, and I feel confident he gave it as presented to the English officials.

It appears that the young Chinaman above alluded to had committed an offence which, under the Chinese laws, was capital, and to save his neck had concealed himself from the officers of justice. For his capture a reward of $1,000 was offered, and the mother, being cognizant of his place of refuge, appealed to him in person after the following manner :

1st. That she was entitled to a support from him, and as then situated he was unable to supply it.

2nd. That the income from the sum offered for his apprehension would support her for the remainder of her life, and hence it was his duty to surrender himself and thus enable her to deliver him to justice and to claim the reward. This he did, and for the offence against the law was decapitated ; the mother received the reward and lived upon its proceeds.

It hardly seems possible that any mother could act in such an inhuman and unnatural way, but unless this officer, as well as all others at headquarters, were imposed upon, which is not very probable, there is every reason for accepting it as a well substantiated fact.

I had been but a few days at Shanghai, when I began making inquiries concerning a trip up the Yangtse Kiang, and learned that it could easily be accomplished by anyone of the three lines of steamers plying between this city and Hankow, a port 600 miles in the interior. Accordingly I started on the morning of March 31st, by the steamboat "*Shanghai*," a river steamer modeled after our North River boats, and having many of the conveniences of our best vessels. First-class passengers are especially well provided for, and have large roomy state-rooms (English cabins).

In passing down the Woosung, which joins the

Yangtse some fourteen miles from this city, I had an excellent opportunity of seeing its shores and the high cultivation which obtains. One of its most striking features is the immense number of mounds, resembling cocks of hay. These are Chinese graves, and, as you may imagine, many are decidedly ancestral. They have been burying in this mode for centuries, as under their Confucian code all ancestral remains must be respected. I could not avoid thinking, as I viewed the effects of private burying grounds in China, that if some of our Long Island friends who have them upon their farms could see what they are liable to come to, they would soon seek some common cemetery for the disposal of the dead.

But to return to the Yangtse. We found its waters very muddy and, like those of the Mississippi, filled with sand-bars, and the channel liable to constant changes—thus calling for great care at many points, in order to follow its channel. The river, at the point we entered it, is several miles in width, but narrowed as we ascended, and the banks increased slightly in height. The shores were highly cultivated, and covered with wheat fields and every variety of vegetable. This wheat, I was told, would be ripe by the end of May, and would give place to some other crop. In some cases they are able to gather, in the twelve months, three good ones. The farmers' huts line the river through much of its course. They are very rude affairs, with only mud walls and thatch-

ed roofs, and no flooring.   The untidy habits of this
class are fully shown by the pigs and chickens run-
ing in and out of the cottages at will.

Fifty five miles from Shanghai we passed the village of Langshan.   There is nothing remarkable about
it, save that the original Langshan breed of black fowl,
much prized in Europe and America, came from there.

One hundred and fifty-six miles above Shanghai
we reached Chinkiang.   This is the first treaty port
on the river ; and, having a good deal of cargo for
that place, we stopped there some hours.

Nanking, the capital of the Empire under the Ming
dynasty, is 200 miles from our starting point, but, as
it is not open to trade, we merely stopped long
enough to discharge the passengers—all Chinese—
who had started with us and receive others on board
from one of their river boats.   The approach to this
city is marked by several pagodas, perched upon high
eminences, and several joss houses.   Its city wall is
also a feature, and is said to measure 21 miles.   It
seemed in a good state of repair.   Like the walls of
most of the Chinese cities, it is crenelated for musket-
try, and has at its back a heavy embankment of earth.
This is one of the cities that suffered heavily during
the Taiping rebellion, which prevailed during a good
portion of the period from 1852 to 1858.

Kiew Kiang, 400 miles up the river, is near some
of the finest scenery.   Just above that city there are
some stretches that would compare favorably with our

Hudson River; but in the main the country is flat, and were it not for the large number of villages, the boat life, and the constant change of scene, the trip would not be especially interesting.

Han-Kow, the end of our up-river journey, was reached on the fourth day from starting. It should not have taken us more than three, but we were heavily loaded and there were other detentions that kept us back. Han-Kow, with its two adjoining cities of Hanyan and Wochan, is put down as containing more than 1,000,000 of people. Some estimate the aggregate as greater, but as I have no means of judging, I accept the former. It is exceedingly difficult to estimate, with any degree of accuracy, a Chinese population, as their towns are built so much more compactly than ours, and the streets are so much narrower. All space is covered over ; but, on the other hand, nearly all the houses are of but one story, and did they not huddle together, their cities would not be so very populous.

I was not sorry to reach the limit of the up-river journey, but I could not avoid exclaiming : " What a mighty river the Yang-tsze is !" for at this distance (600 miles in the interior and very heart of China) there was sufficient depth of water to float the largest ocean steamers, numbers of which load, every tea season, direct for London. Han-Kow is about 100 miles from the tea-growing section, which plant (as in India) is chiefly cultivated on the sides of

13

mountains—much of the land being terraced, the better to protect the plants from washing, through the rains, a large fall of which is essential to tea culture.

At Han-Kow I was introduced to a new industry —the making of brick tea. That is the fine powdered tea and refuse, which, not being salable in European markets, is here, after being moistened, pressed into bricks weighing $2\frac{1}{2}$ pounds, packed into basket crates of 180 pounds each, and shipped to Tientsin, from whence it goes, by pack trains, to Siberia and the remote sections of Russia. This, of course, is an inferior article, but it has grown to be a staple commodity in distant Russia and Thibet, and, in the absence of coin, serves as a medium of exchange. The making of this brick tea is entirely in the hands of Russians, and they form quite a material part of the Han-Kow European colony.

Our return trip enabled us to see points that we had passed at night on our way up—such, for instance, as the mouth of the Grand Canal, which crosses the Yang-tsze near Chin-Kiang, and serves as a great feeder to this river, as it reaches as high up as Pekin, at the north, and to the south near Canton. Besides this, there are a vast number of rivers and many lakes that are tributary to this mighty river, which has a length of over 3,000 miles.

We reached this city, on our return, eight days from the time of departure—pleased with the journey, and feeling that we had gained not a little information by penetrating so far into the interior of the country ; and feeling, also, greatly impressed with the magnitude of this immense river—perhaps the greatest, viewed from all stand-points, in the world.

XX

CHINESE FORTIFICATIONS.

HAN-KOW, CHINA.
(ABOUT LAT. 30° 32′ N., LONG. 114° 19′ E.
TEMP. IN SHADE, 69°.)
April 6th, 1886.

WHEN I closed my letter from India, I rather intimated you might hear from me again at some point farther to the eastward, and I must confess in doing so I had China in my mind. Thinking that in that distant and little explored land there would be some military novelty that I could pick up for the benefit of your readers—something like a guard mount, a parade, or some military procession, or a barrack scene, so different from aught else I've witnessed, that would serve as a real treat to the patrons of the MILITARY SERVICE JOURNAL ;* but I fear my hopes are likely to be thwarted, as three weeks in China have failed to produce anything that seems especially appropriate for a military letter. In truth,

---

* Journal Military Service Institution of the U. S.

I've seen very little of Chinese troops. On my visit
to Canton, an excursion which I made from Hong-
Kong, I had the good fortune to travel with Captain
Lloyd of the steamboat *Han-Kow*, which makes
daily trips between Canton and Hong-Kong, a fine
boat modelled after our North River steamers, and
as roomy and comfortable as could be wished. Captain Lloyd's knowledge of the river, and the various
batteries which have been constructed on the Canton or Pearl River for the defences of the city of
Canton, gave me a good idea of its fortifications,
most of which are of recent construction. The late
unpleasantness between the Chinese and French
frightened them into doing something for their city.
These batteries are evidently well placed, and have
mounted some of the most improved and best constructed modern guns. I think Krupp has supplied
some of the best ; European engineers have evidently been employed in these defences, to which
they add a good system of torpedoes. This scare
has had another good effect, viz., to connect the central government at Pekin with their various provinces and military works by a good system of tele-
graphs. This latter is regarded by the Europeans
as the forerunner of the railway. Both, I believe,
are opposed by the literary and political mandarins,
who desire to keep the people in ignorance and the
power in their own hands ; but nothing would do so
much toward bringing to light the acts of those offi-

cials as a good and rapid system of communications with the various parts of the Empire. One hears from every quarter of the "*squeezes*" of these officials, which are practised as largely in military matters as in their civil callings. I have been told that their military mandarins, who seem to have most arbitrary power, are in the habit of reporting and drawing funds for the payment of a number of troops, sometimes double that which they actually have under their command. Even their great *Li-hung-Chang*, Viceroy of the province of Pe-chi-ti, and with Tien-Tsin as his head-quarters, has been reported as having drawn payment for a much larger number of troops than was actually in service. Such acts could not be successfully carried out if the communication with various sections of the Empire were rapid and frequent.

Notwithstanding such charges, Li-hung-Chang is justly regarded as the great man of the Empire, is more advanced in his views than any other official, and is actually making greater innovations upon the time-honored customs and traditions than any prominent official that China has produced for many years. I believe he favors the introduction of the railroad system and the improvement of roads. At present China has only foot-paths, or such as would only pass for these, between its most important and populous cities. Its commerce for centuries has depended upon its canals and rivers. He is one of the men of whom it is reported General Grant spoke when asked what great men he had met in the course of his tour around the world, and his reply was: " Beaconsfield in England, Gambetta in France, Bismarck in Germany, and *Li-hung-Chang* in China." These *squeezes*, to which I have made reference, are repeated at the central government, and the mandarins who chance to receive good appointments from the Emperor are, at the expiration of their term of office, invited to Pekin to pay their respects to him. And should they fail to grease the palms of his subordinates. some of their weak points will be brought to light, and in place of paying a moderate sum it may cost them many thousands of *taels* to escape with their heads. The Chief Inspector of Trade at Canton holds his appointment for three years. At the time of retiring he visits Pekin on the accustomed visit to the Emperor, and he rarely gets off with less than 100,000 taels (about $142,000), and, besides it, he has probably put away a large fortune for future use, all of which has been made out of a salary of $2,500. I would not repeat these stories had I not heard the same thing from different sources in various parts of China, and from parties whom I have reason to credit.

Another evidence of lack of faith in the honesty of their own officials, is shown in the custom-house system of the country, especially the dues collected from foreign nations. At the close of the last English and French war in China, about 1859, a large indemnity was demanded, but, not having faith in its payment, these Powers claimed the right to collect, through a commission of their own, the dues at certain ports, which was done, they transmitting the surplus to the central government. The latter, finding that the work was so honestly performed and so much more money flowing into the general treasury than before, asked this commission to organize a complete system, covering all the ports of entry throughout the Empire open to foreign trade, which is in force at the present moment. The officer in charge of this system is Sir Robert Hart. This commission has greatly extended its labors, and it now covers a good deal of ground, such as the lighting of the coast and navigable rivers, the police of harbors and rivers, and even the purchase of gunboats for the protection of shipping against pirates. The officials composing this service are made up from all the various nationalities trading with China, the number from each nation being about in proportion to the revenues paid in. The pay is liberal, and the service has called to its aid a most honorable and intelligent body of gentlemen, so that it ranks second only to the civil service of India. Unlike that, it has no pension system attached to it, but, in lieu, a bonus of one year's pay is given its officers at the end of each seven years' service. I believe it is in contemplation to tax the officials and create a fund securely placed, so that in the event of the Chinese government doing away with this system the interest of this fund will serve as a pension to those who may have honorably retired. But I have wandered far from my subject, and must now return to the military items variously picked up.

Respecting the Chinese army as an organized body, I've not been able to learn that such an institution exists. The viceroys governing the various provinces are held responsible for the peace and good order of their respective charges, and it seems to rest with them to call out the local militia to the extent that they deem necessary, and this is largely made up from the coolie class, which is the lowest order in the Chinese social scale, all menial labor falling to their lot. At most all the capitals of the various provinces that I've passed there has been some little display of military, especially at the river ports, and I presume they keep there a certain nucleus into which the drafted men are received, and where they get a certain amount of military instruction. A large display of banners seems an essential feature of all their manœuvres. As I was entering the Woosung River, on my way to Shanghai, the sailors from their gunboats were being landed, presumably for some field exercises, and the number of banners that were in line as they formed on shore was prodigious. I presume they'd soon get over such ideas if engaged in a long war, and when they discovered that such objects served as excellent targets for the enemy.

A trip up this great river has added materially to my information and opened my eyes to the numbers and extent of their river defences, for at numerous points along its course apparently strong earthworks have been erected, and they seem to have shown good judgment in selecting the best sites for its defence, often, however, omitting the important consideration of protecting themselves from an attack in the rear, and forgetting that an enemy is not likely to approach from the direction you are best prepared to resist him.   The earthworks below Nan-Kin furnish an example of this character, and the same may be said of some others.   At many of these military stations we have observed their men idling about, but at scarcely any did we see them engaged in drilling or performing any of the duties of a soldier.   Their dress is precisely the same as any civilian Chinese (colors dark and light blue), and apparently without any marks to identify them as soldiers.   There was an exception to this at one or two of the military works we passed, and at these the dark blue sack or coat had its skirts edged with a broad band of red, with a red badge upon the breast containing the number of the regiment, and I am led to believe that this is the chief distinguishing facing of most of their troops ; it also extends to the retainers of many of the mandarins, as I've observed them in passing through the streets, the mandarin himself being usually borne in a sedan chair. I've used the latter quite frequently, and have found it rather comfortable. About Hong-Kong, which city is built upon the side of a mountain, its use was almost indispensable, the climate being, at the time I visited it, too debilitating to admit of walking up its steep streets. In visiting Chinese cities, I've usually adopted the open sedan chair (with three bearers), in order to avoid the filth of their narrow streets, and also to escape the annoyance of being jostled and surrounded by a crowd of curious men and boys. I passed a portion of yesterday in Han-Kow City, and was glad I had taken this precaution ; for, whenever I entered a shop to make purchases, I had no alternative but submit to their following, and at times must have had more than fifty of them pressing uncomfortably close upon me. However, I submitted with the best grace possible, to the examination of the various articles of my clothing, watch, chain, and the like. In the course of my wanderings through the town, or, to speak more correctly, in my sedan chair-ride, I came upon one of their finest joss-houses, and through the guide asked for permission to enter, which was granted. After inspecting the central court, and the high altar or place where their chief images are kept, and before which they usually burn their joss-sticks and say their prayers, I was asked into an adjoining court, where I found a most respectable assemblage witnessing a theatrical performance. I was given a choice seat, asked to partake of some refreshment, such as tea, melon seeds, preserved fruits and cakes, and treated with every consideration. I naturally inferred that I was to pay for all this attention, but they positively declined any remuneration, and I could only return their hospitality by thanks, which were uttered in English, and, I fear, were poorly understood. I have since learned that it is often the custom for some of their wealthy citizens, especially when members of certain guilds, to entertain their friends in this mode, and this one was given on the anniversary of one of their religious festivals. The host received his guests (all men) at the entrance of the theatre, where he welcomed them by repeated bows, which were returned, neither host nor guests offering to shake hands, but holding them in front with palms together, and when bowing, bringing the chin down close to them. One might almost say that each one shook his own hands, and this, I must conclude, is the fashion in the best Chinese circles, as I've never seen collected a more distinguished-looking set than those occupying the best seats in this theatre.

It was a new experience for me to find the theatre an accompaniment of their religious edifice, but upon enquiry, learned it was quite general with the wealthy class. I watched the performance for more than an hour, and was naturally interested, as it was my first experience. There were no women on the stage, but two were personated by men, whose make-up was so good, even to the pinched small feet, that I was thoroughly deceived as to their sex. And here I propose adding an item, for the benefit of your lady readers, respecting the mode of pinching the feet into the shapeless mass, as we *"foreign devils"* view it, and which so generally obtains with the aristocratic class. It is less practised in the south of China, but, in the north, no mother will permit her daughter to grow up with the feet that naturally belong to the child, as in the eyes of the *"jeunesse dorée"* she would not be a fit subject for their attentions or admiration. This operation, so far as I have been able to learn, begins at an early age, the child not being more than two or three years old. The first step is to bandage the four smaller toes so tightly under the ball of the foot that they are almost buried into the flesh. The next move is to force these up so that they rest in the hollow of the foot, making the whole thing into a lump, and leaving only it, the heel, and big toe, on which to walk. This operation is continued up to the age of fifteen or sixteen, and is attended with intense pain, the screams and moanings of the child bearing testimony to the sufferings it endures, and after the operation is complete they go stamping about much as one would who had lost both feet. There is no elasticity to the walk, and often they have to support themselves by some object. Such is the power of fashion, which is said to have had its origin with some arbitrary ruler, in order to prevent women from gadding. The universal habit of wearing pig-tails by the men is another evidence of the influence of fashion, origi- nally imposed upon the Chinese race by their Tartar conquerors as a symbol of servitude. It has grown to be an essential part of them, and the man con- demned to cut off this appendage regards himself as disgraced.

But to return to the Yang-tsze, on which I've been travelling for the past week. It certainly is a noble river, and probably has tributary to it one of the richest sections of the globe. Its banks are lined with peasants' cottages almost the entire distance from Shanghai to this city, and the population along its entire course, added to that which lives upon the lakes, canals, and rivers that are tributary to it, is estimated at 150,000,000. The soil is very rich, and often produces three crops per year. The largest ocean steamers navigate its waters up to this city, six hundred miles above Shanghai, and, but for the two rapids, heavy-draught vessels could go six hun- dred miles above this. Its entire length is variously stated at between twenty-five hundred and three thousand miles. Its shores bear a strong resemblance to some of our Western rivers, and like them have to be protected from overflows by dikes or artificial embankments. Many of China's most populous cities are situated upon its banks. I mention Chin-Kiang, Nan-king, Wukee, Ngdu-King-Foo, Kiu-Kiang, and this city with its two suburban ones of Han-Yang and Wu-Chang, are placed at over 1,000,000 of inhabitants. Most of the cities are walled, and can only be entered by the gates, where a duty, resembling the octroi of France, is collected. So far as I am able to judge, these walls are in good condition, and are backed by a heavy earthen embankment. That at Han-Kow, I know to be at least twenty feet thick, and I presume many of the others are equally strong. These walls are all crenelated, which produces a pretty effect ; the perimeter of the wall at Nan-king is put at twenty-one miles, and I don't think it exaggerated. The approaches to most of their cities are usually marked by one or more pagodas, and if high ground or an eminence can be found, it is placed on the top ; but the appearance of their towns is far from attractive, houses of a single story, and usually of a sombre-gray color, the most prominent structures being the joss-houses and pagodas, the former with the peculiar concave-shaped ridges and upturned eaves, the effect of which is rather odd and picturesque.

Before closing this rather lengthy epistle, I wish to speak of a very nice and appropriate compliment paid by Captain Selfridge, U. S. Navy, commanding U. S. Steamer *Omaha*, who, on a recent visit of

Major-General Cameron, commanding the British troops in China, turned out his marines and a share of his sailors, and escorted the General to the race-course, where he inspected a body of the Shanghai volunteers. The blue-jackets looked and marched well, and were highly complimented. This act of courtesy struck me as being well placed, and a good promoter of friendly feeling between the two nations, who have so much in common; besides, it gave the captain an opportunity of showing the Chinese that, in addition to his naval guns, he was prepared to land a respectable force, and do some fighting on shore.

XXI

SHANGHAI TO NAGASAKI.

MITSU BISHI, STEAMER YOKOHAMA MARU,
JAPAN WATERS, *April 18th, 1886.*

I AM again afloat, and as you observe, in a veritable Japanese vessel—she forming one of a valuable line running between Shanghai and Yokohama, and having connections in various parts of Japan and Corea. Europeans, however, fill the most important posts, such as captain, chief engineer, and mates, but the working of the ship is with Japanese, who are expert sailors and have had their tuition through the extensive fisheries of this land; for, I imagine, there are few countries with Japan's area that can show such an extended coast line of navigable waters, bays, and inland seas; and, as fish is one of the staple articles of food, the handling of boats in their capacities as fishermen furnishes a good education and fits them for making excellent sailors. I believe for some time after their acquisition of war ships (they have now a far more powerful

14

fleet than our own proud nation can show) some of their ships were commanded by Europeans, but at the present date all their war vessels are in the hands of natives, and a share of the merchants' ships —particularly the cargo boats—are navigated by their own countrymen.

We left Shanghai on the 14th. The morning was a beautiful one, and as we steamed down the Woo-sung River its shores looked exceedingly attractive. Peach, plum, and cherry trees were in blossom, and the leaves of the willow were partly formed. The latter appears to be the prevailing tree along these Chinese rivers, and I saw but little else in my long journey up the Yang-tsze. I can't account for this, save that I've heard that during the Taeping rebellion in China the rebels destroyed most of the forest trees along the line they occupied, and there does not appear to have been any law compelling the planting of others, as obtains in many countries, and which most travellers wish was thoroughly enforced in all— our own being no exception, as we are sadly in need of some well-executed law on this point.

Our two days' journey across the Eastern Sea, separating China from Japan, was a pleasant one, the ship's company agreeable and the waves calm— enabling all to come on deck.

We passed, on the 15th, the large island of Quel-part, which lies directly in the track of vessels run-ning between Shanghai and Japan, and on the even-

ing of that day entered the beautiful harbor of Nagasaki—one of the most picturesque I've ever seen.
It being night, its beauties were not revealed to us
till the next morning, when we awoke. The town
was just opposite, and our anchorage so near shore
as to enable us to recognize friends passing along
the " bund." This term, which I first heard in India,
is applied to the water-fronts of the various foreign
"concessions" throughout the East. It is usually
a broad space in front of the European residences,
planted with one or more rows of trees. Its face is
protected from the washing of the waters by a stone
wall, and it serves as an admirable lounging place for
the foreign element. It is also an excellent play-
ground for their children—the natives only visiting
it when called there by business.

We were some twenty-four hours in the port of
Nagasaki—time which was industriously employed
by all, particularly the new-comers, who were eager
to see all that was novel in this most interesting
country. In spite of a pouring rain, we were early
on shore and visiting the various shops. Porcelain
and tortoise-shell shops were the most attractive to
me, and at one of the latter I purchased two excellent miniature copies, in shell, of the native boats
and jinrickishaws. There is an extensive bazaar,
filled with every variety of native productions, that
I was much interested in, and that consumed a share
of the rainy morning. The afternoon was fine, and

we profited by it in wandering over the hills and through their principal park, where we saw our first Japanese temple. We also visited one or two tea houses. These are attractive places—the ladies of the house coming out to meet and welcome us. There is no shaking of hands, but they make most graceful bows, smiling all the while, and welcoming us by kindly words, which, I'm sorry to say, I did not understand.

I was aided, however, by a friend, Mr. Hunt, long a Japanese resident, who was kind enough to explain what the young waitresses were saying. After taking a cup of tea, which is offered without milk or sugar, and in tiny cups, we bid them good-by, receiving in return the most profound bows, which they made while kneeling—the head being brought almost down to the floor. This form of politeness is striking, and the new comer to this picturesque land at once remarks upon it. It is as common to see two of the peasant or working class, when passing each other on the street, stop and make a low bow, as with us for the best class to raise their hats. This courtly demeanor of all classes toward each other at once attracts, and when it is coupled with a kindly smile and every evidence of good feelings, you conclude they are the most polite people in the world, and are naturally led to ask whence it arises. The guide books tell us that it is taught through their religion and a national regard for etiquette which is held in high esteem. Their religion inculcates the reverence to parents as one of the highest of virtues, and to it as much as any one cause may be traced the foundation of such universal politeness.

Continuing our walk through the park to which I've alluded, we could not help admiring the beautiful cherry blossoms, which, although late for this portion of Japan, were still in considerable numbers. and which the Japanese so greatly admire that almost all grounds have a share of them. The fruit of this species is small and hardly edible, and the tree is grown chiefly for the beauty of its blossoms. One of their most popular out-of-door festivals is held when these trees are in full flower.

In the course of our wanderings, and at a point in the park commanding one of the finest views of the city and harbor, we came upon a stone slab erected to commemorate the visit of Gen. Grant, U. S. Army, to this hospitable town, when he and his good wife each planted a tree. The slab bears the following inscription, which is an exact copy of the General's well-known hand, and with which I was for many years familiar (as I served for eight years as a subaltern in the same regiment), and I could not but remark upon the faithfulness of the copy, which is thus :

" NAGASAKI, JAPAN, *June 23d, 1879.*

"At the request of Governor Watsumi Tada Kalemi, Mrs. Grant and I each planted a tree in the Nagasaki Park. I hope that both trees may prosper, grow large, live long, and their growth and prosperity and long life be emblematic of the future of Japan. U. S. GRANT."

The above is followed by the same sentiment in Japanese characters. One of these trees is dead—possibly the one planted by the General. The other, on the left of the tablet, facing the harbor, is about 15 feet high and apparently doing well. It was not in leaf, being of rather a late species and of the variety known to the Japanese as *Kiri*—botanically *Paulownia Imperialis*. A branch of this tree, with its flower—a light purple one—forms one of the emblems on the reverse side of the coin of the empire. It was, I understand, the crest of the Shoguns during the military reign of that class of monarchs, and is found on the doors and friezes of their temples. The chrysanthemum is the crest of the Mikado, and it now has first place in the various decorations, and since the revolution of 1868, when he became the temporal as well as spiritual head of the empire, no other emblem has been used on public edifices. I will add that the *Kiri* is much prized by the Japanese as a cabinet wood, being light and durable. Many of the boxes that one sees in Japanese shops are made from it.

On modern buildings, especially those of a national character, the chrysanthemum is the only crest, and one finds it on almost all the post-offices, halls of justice, telegraph and municipal buildings. The soldiery and police wear it as a species of button on the bands of their fatigue caps, and not associated with the Shogun crest—doubtless showing that the Mikado is determined to rule alone and not as formerly, when the Daimios and Shoguns controlled the political affairs of the nation.

Before quitting the harbor of Nagasaki I must remark upon the little island of Deshima, which was assigned by the Japanese to the Dutch Trading Company, and for 200 years they were confined to this narrow bit of land, 600 feet in length by 200 in width. It was connected with the town by two stone bridges, which were, however, carefully guarded, and its residents were never permitted to enter the city. Their trading vessels were admitted to the factory through water-gates, which were kept closed. Only a privileged few, with the officials, had access to the island. The Dutch were forbidden bringing their families, and only a few loose women were permitted to have intercourse with the sailors and factory men. I presume it was then that these women were taught the dance known as "Jon-kino," which is exceedingly indecent and immoral in its character. This dance begins by taking out their hair-pins, and throwing off, in turn, each article of dress, till not a stitch is left to lay aside. The dance is now prohibited by law, and it can only be given surreptitiously. The ordinary dance of the Ghesa, or dancing girls, consists mainly of a series of posturings, and is as modest as the most scrupulous could wish.

We left Nagasaki at midnight on the 17th, and had a good passage, reaching the Straits of Simonisaki about midday, and came to anchor off the town of the same name.   These straits separate the island of Kiu-Shiu from that of Nippon, or the main island of Japan, and here begins what is called the Inland Sea—that famous body of inland water, nearly 300 miles in length, and navigable for ocean-going steamers, that has no equal in my experience, and possibly is not excelled in any section of the globe, for beauty and the picturesque.

We were some three hours taking in a supply of rice—some 1,000 sacks of one pecul each (133⅓ pounds).   The sacks, or coverings, were entirely composed of straw, but so completely made that I did not observe the slightest leakage of the grain, and yet there was no inner covering of cotton or gunny cloth.

The straits are something less than one-half a mile wide at their narrowest part, and being surrounded by high mountains, are capable of being easily defended; and they have been the scene of numerous encounters.

Near this point we caught our first glimpse of the Tokaido—a national road leading along, or near, the coast as far as the capital—Tokio (Yeddo), some 600 miles away.   It seemed well constructed, and, when running near the sea, was protected by a wall of stone.   The roadway was apparently not more than fifteen feet wide.

"The Inland Sea," as it is generally styled, consists of a succession of seas and narrow straits, separating the main islands from each other; and these large bodies of water are known on Japanese charts as, 1st, " Suwo Nada;" 2d, " Iyo Nada ;" 3d, " Bingo Nada;" 4th, " Harima Nada," and "Isumi Nada." The islands are most numerous near the narrower points of the channel, and of the 3,000 that belong to Japan a goodly number are to be found in this inland sea. The North Channel, as it is termed, and which we reached early this morning, has some of the finest scenery to be found in the entire length of this beautiful sail. Here the ship skirts along the base of bold mountains (many evidently the remains of extinct volcanoes), the sides of which are clothed in verdure, and often terraced and cultivated up to their very summits. I counted the terraces on one of these mountains, and they exceeded thirty—all sustained by solidly-built walls of stone. One sees, too, picturesque villages hid away, as it were, in narrow ravines; the straw-thatched roofs, coming almost down to the ground, form a pretty feature of this interesting trip. There were also *Shinto* temples and shrines, embowered in groves of trees, sometimes perched upon the highest peaks, but always so placed as to give a pretty effect to the picture. As the day was fine, we watched for hours this ever-varied, but never-tiring, scene, and were rather sorry when, about 4 P. M., it was announced that Kobe was in sight. We entered its pretty little

harbor before sunset, and steamed quite close up to
the "bund" of the European Concession, which is
handsomely laid out, and bordered by the homes of
the foreign colony, which are usually square wooden
structures, with good wide porches and galleries.
We were soon on shore and comfortably housed at
the "Hiogo Hotel," where this letter must close.

XXII

KOBE TO KIOTO.

YA-AMI HOTEL, KIOTO, JAPAN,
(LAT. 34. 30 N., LONG. 135 E.; TEMP. 50 .)
April 24th, 1886.

KIOTO seems very properly to deserve the good reputation it bears among most travellers, as one of the choice places in Japan. Located at the head of a rich valley,—in fact the city extends well up the sides of a mountain, bountifully supplied by several streams of water, which come directly from the adjacent mountains, and connected with the coast by a well-conducted railway,—there are few spots where one is more disposed to linger than this. The city itself is very attractive. Being for many centuries the seat of the Imperial Government, and at a time when the Mikado was regarded as the spiritual head of the nation, it naturally attracted thither the best talent of the country, and the remains of their work are found in the ornaments and decorations of its temples, and the skill of its workmen in various forms of art.

It may be well to state that passports are still required from those who wish to travel to the interior, and away from the treaty ports. Hence, before setting out on my journey to this city I secured in advance, through the U. S. Minister at Tokio, a passport which designated the various districts of Japan that I wished to visit. It is well to make a note of this, as travellers are sometimes turned back and subject to great delays. The railway ticket agents require passports to be shown before issuing tickets, and hotel proprietors will not entertain you unless you can produce one.

The situation of this hotel is especially good, being at one of the highest points in the city,—in fact, it may properly be called a suburb,—and commanding a superb view of the entire town, a good share of the valley, and the high mountains opposite. Japanese, like the Chinese, cities do not furnish much that is admirable in the way of house architecture—the buildings being usually of one or one and a half stories and with little decoration to relieve the monotony of the tiled roofs and rather bare walls. The latter are, however, varied by wooden lattice work, which in some cases forms the outside protection of the sliding paper windows of the inside, and are separated from the former by a considerable interval. In many instances there is still another outside covering, especially to the lower story. This is formed by a series of board frames that slide in grooves in the upper and lower galleries, and are securely fastened. By day these are put into a small closet, especially designed for them, and the operation of opening the windows in the early morning is likely to arouse the most profound sleeper, and possibly to call forth some savage remarks from the tired traveller, as personal experience on my part can attest.

It seems very odd to live in a city where glass is scarcely used, and where light is admitted by the aid of translucent paper. Still it has its advantages, and I recall, that at one hotel, the dining-room windows of which one had become a little torn—going out for a short walk I found on my return that the proprietor had put in an entire new set, and he could not have consumed more than an hour in doing it. Even the partitions of the rooms are often made of paper, and the parts of these partitions so slide within each other that each floor is capable of being converted into a single apartment. The shops do not differ materially from the private dwellings. In truth, the shop and habitable rooms so run into each other that it is difficult to say which is the real family residence. I observe that the most valuable goods are usually kept in the upper stories, and when there is anything choice and rich to be exhibited you are often invited to the upper rooms, which are reached by a narrow stairway leading directly up from the shop below. In my wanderings about these establishments I often happen upon a neat little kitchen, fitted up with the tiniest of charcoal ranges, and it is delightful to see with what good nature the lady of the house submits to my rather prying disposition to examine the various cooking utensils, cupboards, etc., all of which are kept scrupulously neat and clean. Their apartments, covered with the newest of matting, are alike neatly kept. One is usually asked to remove their shoes and accept of a pair of sandals when entering the living rooms. As foreigners generally wear some sort of foot covering that is not readily removed, an exception is usually made in their favor, but I believe never with their own country people.

Upon entering the temples we also are compelled to observe this rule, and travellers often provide themselves with linen or cotton covers that can be slipped over the leather shoe, and thus save time and trouble. Sandals, or clogs, are almost universally worn by the natives, and are kept on by the use of straps or thongs passing between the big toe and its neighbor and over the instep to the sides of the sandal. The better to effect this, the stocking, which is almost invariably of white material, is so made that the big toe fits into a separate part.

One feature of their house architecture, which is especially striking, is the entire absence of chimneys or anything approaching them. In many of the residences there appears to be a species of ventilator along the ridge, but no sign of a chimney. Their chief mode of warming themselves is from a kind of brazier filled with coals, and you will find them sitting for hours over this highly-polished heater, occasionally smoking a pipe and chatting. I'm inclined to think that the lack of erectness in their carriage is due to this constant stooping over this little furnace of theirs. In the far North, where the cold is intense, they burn fuel in a species of oven, which warms the apartments, or else they make use of large metal pots, hung in the centre of the room— the smoke passing out through the ridge of the roof. There is no lack of fuel, as in China and India, where, as I've before noticed, the droppings of animals, mixed with straw and sun-dried. constitute the largest share of their cooking material. Why it has never occurred to the rather active brains of this people to construct some sort of chimney I can't well understand. Another mode of keeping warm is to put on additional clothing, the natural effect of which is to add materially to the bulkiness of their appearance. The children, under their three or four jackets, as I've sometimes seen them, look very funny. Infants are almost invariably carried on the backs of mothers or young girls. and are strapped on almost the same as I've seen among the North American Indians. They seem to have the best of tempers, as I have not, up to the present writing, heard any cries from them.

Since writing these lines a friend has suggested that this lack of erectness in the women is due to their always having had to carry something on their backs. The youngest girls of the family take care of the babies by having them strapped to their backs, and it is as common to see a girl of five or six with a baby strapped on her back as to see the child herself; and when the baby shows signs of uneasiness she quiets it by raising herself quite rapidly up and down on her toes and heels, which produces a similar effect to dancing the child in one's arms.

Their temples are much the largest of the various edifices that one sees in or about the city. The approach to them is usually marked by a stone or wooden gateway. Once within this, you pass through a line of stone lanterns, and possibly come upon another gateway, or smaller shrine, before reaching the main temple ; and after ascending several steps, you enter upon the body of the building, where are placed the high altar and the sacred image before which the people offer their prayers—the petitioner usually beginning prayer by clapping his hands, as it were to call the attention of the god to his supplications. In some instances bells or gongs are hung at the entrance, which are sounded previous to commencing prayer.

Probably the most noticeable, as well as the most interesting, of all the temples about Kioto is the Nishi Hongwanji, where in olden times the nobles of the court and high functionaries worshipped. It has attached to it extensive apartments, decorated by the best artists of the times—the subjects being usually some characteristics of Japanese life. Some of these rooms, or audience-chambers, are really very handsome. The Hondo, or principal building, of this Buddhist temple is 138 feet in length by 93 in depth, and the floor covers an area of 477 Japanese mats. I did not learn the exact size of a mat, but judged it to be about 3 feet square. One is struck in this, as in many other of their places of worship, by the great resemblance of the high altar, incense-burners, candlesticks, etc. (all of which are accompaniments of these temples), to those of the Roman Catholic churches. Even the priests that one sees about them and in the streets dress in a similar manner, except that the Japanese priests shave their heads completely, and not alone the crown, as obtains with many Roman priests.

This hotel seems to be especially favored with churches, as there are some three or four in our immediate vicinity. To one belongs an enormous bell, which is sounded every morning at daylight, and of which we have full benefit. However, as its tone is excellent, I can't say that it disturbs me. In form it resembles the Chinese, being of cupola shape and tongueless. The sound is produced by striking a circular boss, moulded for the purpose, upon the outer surface of the bell with a heavy oscillating

15

beam suspended by a rope. It requires eight men to work this beam, and they give the bell eighty strokes each morning. It usually awoke me, but its tone was so soft and musical, that I did not object in the least to lying awake and listening to it. This only goes on during the festival season, which, for the want of the Japanese name, is usually called the " cherry blossom " one. It opens with the first appearance of those flowers and lasts till they have fallen. It is a species of wild cherry, and is valued alone for its flowers, which are very large and beautiful. It does bear a small fruit, but I hear it is hardly edible.

This seems to be the season for general merrymaking, as all the theatres and places of amusement are crowded, the country people flocking in to swell the number. There is a species of ballet now going on that has attracted all the Europeans. I've seen it twice. It lasts about half an hour, when the curtain falls and the house is emptied for another audience, when precisely the same thing is repeated. There are some seven of these given in the course of an evening. It can hardly be called a ballet, but is rather a series of posturings, in which fans and wreaths of flowers are freely used. I believe this is the only city where such a representation is given. The dresses are of very decided colors—blue and red predominating—and the usual amount of powder and paint that generally adorns the young Japanese lady is used in this dance. The orchestra, also made up of women, is a feature of the performance. They sing during the dance, and accompany themselves with a species of guitar, and odd-shaped drums and small gongs. I believe that Gilbert and Sullivan have introduced in their opera of "The Mikado" something of this ballet.

In addition to some of the attractions I've enumerated, and which render Kioto such a desirable city to visit, I can add numerous excursions by rail and jinrickishaw. That to Nara, a two days' trip, where the largest bronze *Buddha* in Japan can be seen, as also some fine mountain scenery, is most enjoyable. Then there are the rapids—partly made by jinrickishaw and partly by boat. The descent of these rapids, which are very numerous through a course of some seven miles, is very exciting, and exhibits great skill on the part of the boatmen in managing their boats. The scenery along the river is grand, and with an early morning start, by the time you reach the foot of the rapids you are quite prepared for the comfortable lunch that is spread for you in one of the native tea houses. Our trip was made with a jolly party of six, and we considered the day as well passed.

These country excursions are profitable in other ways, throwing one in contact with the people, and enabling you to form an idea of how they live, etc. We passed on the road many of them coming to the city with various descriptions of produce, and their different methods of transporting it were striking. A favorite one seemed to be in long two-wheeled carts, either drawn by men or bullocks. The roads being very narrow, only very narrow-gauged—say two feet—carts can be used. Another very common mode was to pack it upon bullocks, which are driven by a cord attached to a ring in the animal's nose. Nearly all the bullocks were shod with straw sandals as a protection to their feet over mountain roads, and my guide informed me that it was only recently that the Japanese had even taken to shoeing their horses, of which they have a very limited number. I've only seen, in this city of some 225,000 people, about half a dozen very shabby-looking ponies. I don't know what I shall find elsewhere, but certainly horses are not numerous here.

The trip to Otsu, a pretty town on Lake Biwa, which is the largest lake in Japan—some thirty-seven miles in length and navigated by steamers—proved a very agreeable one, and is easily made by rail in an hour. The scenery along the line is bold and picturesque. On the way you pass through numerous tea fields and much good farming country, which is cultivated to the greatest perfection. Many of the tea gardens were protected by straw mats on bamboo poles. This is done for the purpose of forcing the young tea shoots, which furnish the earliest and best teas. You may imagine that labor is cheap where such methods are employed. I inquired and learned that the ordinary laborer gets twenty cents per day and finds himself; best carpenters, seventy-five cents; ordinary ones, sixty cents; and so on down the scale. While speaking of mechanics, I will add that the owners of this hotel are building an addition to the same, which has given me an opportunity of examining their various implements of the trade, many of which would astonish " Boss Terry," our favorite South Side builder ; and perhaps their method of using them more so—as, for example, the Japanese in planing never pushes the tool from him, but draws it toward the body—and in many instances, especially where he has to plane the edge of a board, he stands it upright and pulls the plane down, such an affair as a carpenter's bench not being dreamed of. And yet they do very neat work, and finish off mouldings very handsomely with exceedingly simple tools. Their hours of labor are much the same as with us—that is, they begin work at 7 A. M., take an hour at mid-day for dinner, and "knock off" about 6 P. M.—but I hardly think they work as industriously as our mechanics.

As a people I should say that they were very fond of merry-making, and managed to take a good many holidays. One sees, too, great crowds in the street that do not appear to be doing anything, and you are apt to infer they do not over-work. But as I see but few beggars, and those chiefly young children who ask for pennies, I'm equally inclined to conclude that they labor sufficiently to secure the necessities of life. They certainly are a most good-natured and polite race ; even the commonest peasant will give you a bow that would grace the drawing-room of any nationality, and it is usually accompanied by a smile, and probably a kind word—certainly one if you address him. Of course, in remote districts, where foreigners are rarely seen, they are likely to exhibit some curiosity, and are inclined to gather about if you stop on the streets, and, maybe, examine any article of dress or jewelry ; but it is all done in a most polite matter, and you can't well take offence. They are nothing like as pushing as the Chinese, who would crowd about in a manner that was far from pleasant—especially in view of their untidy habits. The Japanese, on the other hand, is very cleanly in his person, and one can push through a dense crowd without discomfort or observing any unpleasant odor rising from their bodies.

But to return to the town of Otsu and the lake on which it is situated, which, the guide-book tells us, takes its name from a fancied resemblance in its outline to a Chinese guitar. Legend also says that it owes its origin to an earthquake which occurred at a very early period—the same one bringing their famous mountain, " Fuji," to the surface.

I'd like to remain longer in this beautiful place, and examine more closely some of its varied attractions, but time rather presses, and, further, my travelling companions have gone ahead, which is another reason for shortening the stay. Hence I return to-morrow by rail to Kobe, and from there take steamer direct for Yokohama. This city is some two and one-half hours, by rail, from Kobe—the line passing through a highly-cultivated farming district, which at present is largely covered with barley and wheat—the former grain being much used, especially when the rice crop is short. I wish our American farmers could have a peep at Japanese cultivation—it is so thorough and neatly done. Night-soil is much used as a fertilizer—this, mixed with other materials, being the chief mode of enriching the land. This railroad passes through the large city of Osaka, a town on the coast above Kobe, where I shall pass a few hours. It, like this city, is well supplied by canals, the water of which is drawn from the river ; and this method of transporting various products greatly reduces the cost, besides relieving the streets from bulky and cumbersome articles of merchandise. The streets of Japanese cities almost invariably cross each other at right angles, and are laid out with great regularity. No one need get lost if they have any idea of the points of the compass, or have taken the slightest pains to form some plan of the city where they may chance to be stopping.

XXIII

YOKOHAMA TO NIKKO.

*SUZUKI'S HOTEL OR TEA HOUSE, NIKKO
(SUN'S BRIGHTNESS), JAPAN, May 18th, 1886.*

THERE is a Japanese saying, " Until you have seen Nikko don't say 'Kekko'"—grand or splendid.   Of course, I was not one to disregard this proverb, and shortly after my arrival at Yokohama decided on a visit to this sacred spot and the tombs of two of Japan's important and renowned Shoguns, viz., Iye-yasu and Iye-mitsu.   There are several ways of reaching it, but I naturally followed the modern one of railroad, omnibus, and jinrickishaw. It was formerly made solely by jinrickishaw, and occupied several days ; it can now be accomplished in a single day, if a very early start is made from Yokohama ; but I took it leisurely and made a halt of two days at Tokio (Yeddo), and saw a share of the sights of the Japanese capital.   Still, I'm not going to tell you of these now, but reserve them for a future letter.

As the trip to Nikko was likely to involve that of a visit to other points of the empire, and consume several days, I naturally secured the services of a Japanese guide, who was also able to fill the position of cook—an important one on an excursion of this character, as Japanese food only can be secured at the tea houses of the interior; and unless one is prepared to live solely upon vegetables, rice, and fish, with an occasional chicken and eggs, some provision must be made for excursions which take you more than a day's journey from European food and hotels. Mr. and Mrs. Scobell, of Gloucester, England, agreeable and interesting travelling companions of mine in the East, had recently made this excursion, and they warmly recommended a guide called Hakodate, whose services I secured, and he proved worthy of their commendation—being a bright, active fellow, with lots of endurance, always ready for work, and full of resources. He had written recommendations from various parties, but I laid more stress upon one from some American naval officers, who had recently gone over the route, and they warmly praised his usefulness, together with his economical expenditures for the journey. I left to his judgment the purchasing of the various canned articles that he regarded necessary, insisting, however, that he should lay in a certain amount of soft wheaten bread, and several pounds of boiled ham—an article which I've always found fills a most important place and can be called in on most occasions to fill up a gap. He spoke English fairly well, and knew the route thoroughly, having been over it four times this year.

Leaving Yokohama by rail, in something less than an hour we reached Tokio (Yeddo), where we joined a party consisting of General James H. Wilson, of cavalry fame during our Rebellion, and Mr. D. Stevens. The latter, although an American, holds a desirable position in the Japanese diplomatic service, and from his familiarity with the Japanese language, added to his intimate knowledge of much of the country, proved a most valuable acquisition, as well as being a jolly good fellow. He added a servant from his well-supplied household at Tokio, as, also, a goodly quantity of stores. I have also to thank him for much hospitality extended during my two days' stay in the Japanese capital.

All preparations having been completed, we started by rail on a bright, fresh morning for Utsunomiya, distant about 70 miles from Tokio. The line runs through a level country, which at the time was filled with barley and wheat, much of which was nearly ripe. The road passes for a good portion of the way along the valley of the Yeddogawa River, and crosses the Tonegawa at or near Kurikaski. The bridge is not yet complete—hence we were pulled across in a flat boat and changed to another train on the opposite side. Continuing our journey, the line passes, at various points, in sight of the Oshinkaido, one of the national piked roads of the empire, along the borders of which are planted pines and cryptomeria—some of the latter of enormous size. The train reached Utsunomiya about mid-day, and we were at once driven to the Incyd Tea House, where lunch was taken, and then, in a species of omnibus or wagonette, started for Nikko.

The drive for the entire distance is a beautiful one, through an avenue of cryptomeria, a species of cedar, many of which are over 200 years old and of great size. We passed on the way several villages and made two halts for change of horses. The portion of the road from Utsunomiya is called the Rei-pei-shi Kai-do, and is the one along which the representative of the Mikado travelled in his annual visits to the shrine of Iyeyasu. The following explains the name : " (rei) envoy (shi) sent to offer presents (pei) at the chapel in front of the tomb." Kaido means road. At Imaichi, some seven miles from Nikko, it is joined by another national road— also lined with cryptomeria—coming from the west. The effect where these two splendid avenues of trees unite is very fine indeed. I measured the diameter of one of the largest of these trees near its base, and found it over 30 feet.

At Imaichi we found, lining the road, a regiment of cavalry and one of infantry. They were evidently just in from a march, and had halted for a rest or preparatory to bivouacking for the night. The cavalry men were mounted on the native horse of the country—a small animal of 12 or 13 hands, generally entire and capable of a good deal of hard work. They were in good flesh, and both men and horses appeared as if they were well looked after. An officer of the French service, who is in Government employ, was with them, and I understand he was there for the purpose of instructing them in the various arms of the military service, and also in what is equally important—the best method of marching and caring for troops while on the march. We halted at Suzuki's Hotel, or Tea House, at 5 P. M., having driven the distance of 22 miles in less than four hours, which was remarkably good, considering the small, light ponies that drew us and the load —five grown men. So well pleased were we that the driver was rewarded by a respectable *pour boire*, for which he was exceedingly grateful. The remainder of the afternoon was consumed in a walk about the suburbs of Nikko and along the banks of the rushing Daiyagawa, which has all the characteristics of a bold mountain stream, and the deposit of débris near the town is proof positive that in high water it must assume the characteristics of a torrent.

At 7 P. M. we sat down to dinner with appetites that fully prepared us to do justice to the very comfortable and nicely-served meal that Hakodate had gotten up. First came a course of soup, followed by some mountain trout that our provider had picked up. These were followed in turn by some substantial dishes, to all of which we did ample justice. We retired early. This being one of my first experiences in a tea house, I felt somewhat concerned as to how I should fare in the way of a bed; but my guide having taken the precaution of bringing along a pair of sheets, I found, on entering the sleeping apartment, a most comfortable one on the floor—made up of a number of Japanese comforters, which are heavily wadded, and make a very soft bed. There are no bedsteads in Japanese houses—hence the necessity of sleeping on the floor. As an additional precaution, the sheets were sprinkled with flea-powder, but I'm fully of the opinion that this was unnecessary, nor did I find any in the houses that I afterwards occupied ; but I'm told, on good authority, that in midsummer they are abundant and very annoying.

Having a busy day before us, we were aroused quite early, and, taking a good hearty breakfast, set out to inspect the famous shrines and tombs, which were chiefly the objects of our visit. Almost the first interesting object that one meets on leaving the tea house is the sacred bridge, called in Japanese Mihashi. It is rather graceful, built of wood, and painted red, and spans the Daiyagawa River. Its chief importance grows out of a legend that is attached to it. One of the holy men of Japan, who visited Nikko many years since, reached this stream, which at the time was a raging torrent. Not being able to cross, he fell on his knees and earnestly prayed to Buddha and the gods for assistance. In answer to his petition the god appeared on the opposite bank, holding two green and red snakes, which he cast into the torrent, and immediately a bridge was seen to span the stream, and the holy man and his followers crossed in safety. It is closed to the general public, and in former times only the Shoguns and pilgrims were permitted to cross it.

The view up the valley of the river from the public bridge, near at hand, is very fine, and one delights to linger in this vicinity at the close of the day. This view is a favorite one with photographers, and one finds it in almost every collection of Japanese scenery.

Crossing the bridge and continuing our walk through a well-paved avenue, bordered by splendid cedars, we reached the residence of the Shinto priests, who have charge of the tombs and shrines. We were invited in, and passed some time in examining some printed and worked scrolls, which contained incidents in the life of their great Shogun, Iyeyasu—one who had been instrumental in quelling the various dissensions in the Empire, and who, by his firm government, was able to administer the laws of the nation, and to keep the Daimios, or feudal lords, in quietude. He was canonized after death, and hence Nikko became a pilgrimage to the loyal and faithful.

Continuing our rounds, we proceeded to the broad and paved avenue, which leads to some steps. Ascending these, we pass under the granite torii, which is nearly twenty-eight feet high, and the diameter of its columns more than three feet. On the left was a wooden pagoda, which is exceedingly graceful and beautifully painted. If my memory is correct, it is of five stories. The signs of the Japanese zodiac adorn the lower story. Passing on, and ascending a few steps more, we pass through the " Gate of the Two Kings." In this court are some beautiful storehouses, painted a bright red, containing the utensils used at the ceremonies in honor of Iyeyasu, and the furniture and other articles used by that hero during his lifetime ; observing, as we pass on, a fine holy-water cistern of gray granite, made from a single block, with granite columns supporting its roof : all are worthy of notice. After this we came to the bell tower, of handsome workmanship, and near it a bronze candelabra; also a bell presented by the King of Corea. Then, continuing our walk, we ascend some steps and come upon a superb chapel, an apartment of which was devoted to the use of the Shogun. In this we were permitted to examine some of the precious relics of the great man—such as his sword, armor, etc. In this chapel I observed that some of the ornaments represented the flower of the peony (Buddha is usually represented as seated on the lotus). At numerous points about these various shrines and altars we saw the crest of the Shogun, which consists of three leaves—I believe those of the Kiri (*Paulownia Imperialis*), which has a purple flower, not unlike, in appearance, that of the wisteria, only the flower stalks, instead of hanging down, shoot upwards.

Passing out of the last chapel court and ascending a flight of 200 stone steps, we came upon the tomb of the great hero, which is of bronze, of cylindrical form, and surmounted by a graceful cap. Before it, on a low stone table, is an immense bronze stork, holding a brass candle, a bronze incense-burner, and a vase with artificial lotus flowers. Two amainu (heavenly dogs) stand guard near by. One of the great features of this tomb and its adjuncts is the superb manner in which it is located—being on the side of a mountain and surrounded by as beautiful and grand old trees (cryptomeria) as I've ever seen. The shrine and tomb of Iyemitsu is some little distance from that of his grandfather, and is, perhaps, not quite as rich in some of its details; still, it is very fine, and we were conducted through every part; but I will not tire you with a detailed description. We were some four hours making the rounds, and at the end quite ready for lunch, which was in waiting. This disposed of, we made arrangements for continuing our journey to Lake Chiu-zen-ji.

But before leaving Nikko I must speak of its attractions as a summer resort. Already the British minister and some members of the Legation have arranged for passing the hot months there, and I believe there are other Europeans who will join them. Its elevation (2,000 feet) above the sea, added to the numerous picturesque walks and excursions in the neighborhood, renders it particularly attractive to those who wish to escape the heat and impure atmosphere of the crowded cities.

The route from Nikko to Lake Chiu-zen-ji was along and up the valley of the Daiyagawa, and is a pretty steep climb for a share of the way. Realizing this, I had directed Hakodate to secure me a saddle horse, which proved to be a black stallion pony, without any very malicious tricks that I discovered, except, perhaps, the habit he occasionally had of stopping and refusing to proceed further until the betto (horse tender or groom) had turned him around two or three times, when he would continue the journey. The other gentlemen of the party, being younger and rather proud of their climbing powers, made the journey on foot—a distance of some ten miles. The road crosses the river at several points, on rather shaky and unprotected bridges; still I stuck to my pony, and he proved worthy of my confidence. The views along some of the mountain gorges were superb, and at one or two places they included some pretty water-falls, and the

16

mountain sides were covered with a delicate pink azalia, adding greatly to the beauty of the scene. I also saw, on the way, several varieties of trees common to our own latitude, such as the birch, oak, chestnut, maple, and some handsome specimens of the elm. I was told the stream abounded in trout, the best evidence of which were some fine specimens that we had that evening for dinner. We reached the lake about 6 P. M., and, travelling along its border for something less than a mile, came upon the village of the same name, and halted at the Komeya, a comfortable tea house with rooms over-looking the lake. It is one of the few houses occupied at this season—most of the others being closed and open only in August, when the faithful pilgrims resort here in great numbers to bathe in the lake and worship at a favorite temple. Nan-tai-zan, a sacred mountain some 8,000 feet above the sea, borders the lake, and before retiring for the night my companions made arrangements for a guide to ascend it, which they accomplished before break-fast the next morning—a sharp climb of 5,000 feet, the lake being over 3,000 feet above the sea.

We left Chiu-zen-ji in the morning after breakfast, and crossed the lake in one of the native boats. This pull of something more than a mile was a charming one. The waters were beautifully clear and placid, and reflected in the most perfect manner the mountains which border the lake, as also the beautiful azalias, which were in perfection. Gen. Wilson, having a good pair of lungs, produced some wonderful echoes that were repeated more than once. This lake reminded me of that beautiful body of water in Austria, not far from Salzburg, called the Koenig Sea. After crossing the lake, we struck into a mountain path which, after a sharp climb of about half a mile, brought us to the top of the divide and near the source of one of the tributaries of the Watarassegawa. The view from this divide was splendid, and we lingered for a few moments to admire it, and then began, by a zigzag path, the descent. The declivity is very great, and the path difficult—being for a part of the way along the bed of the stream, filled with boulders and sharp stones. We passed, on the way, numerous charcoal pits, the coal from which was intended for the copper smelting works below, which we passed later in the day. The charcoal laborers were powerful men, and we saw them staggering under some enormous loads. After about one hour's walk down the mountain the path began to widen, and soon after we came upon our jinrickishaws, which we had directed to meet us. Most of the party were glad to exchange for this less fatiguing mode of travel. I had before my two-wheeled carriage two splendid specimens of men, who took good care of me during much of the journey of that day.

The trip down the valley of the Watarassegawa is

very fine indeed, and in the course of its numerous windings one has some splendid views. The river at some places takes some bold leaps, forming pretty waterfalls that enliven the scene.

We passed, during the day, numerous villages and through large groves of mulberry trees, where the silk-worm is extensively grown. Lower down in the valley I examined their method of feeding the worms, which simply consists of placing them in large wicker baskets that are arranged on bamboo shelves. In the first stage of their growth the mulberry leaves are chopped up for the young worms, and a proper temperature kept up by the use of charcoal heaters. When sufficiently large the entire leaf is fed to them. All this work is carried on in the cottages of the peasant farmers, and not, as some might suppose, in establishments especially set apart for the culture of the silk-worm. It requires some forty-five or fifty days for the worm to reach the stage where he begins forming the cocoon.

We lunched about noon at Ashiwo and, continuing down the river, halted, about 6 P. M., for the night at Omama—at a tea house called Tsutuya. Hakodate, with his usual foresight, had taken the precaution of sending our baggage on in advance, and had secured for us the best quarters in the village. As the day's journey had been a severe one, we were rather glad when the guide announced that our next day's journey would be a short one. We

JIN-RICK-SHAW. JAPAN.

therefore took it leisurely, and did not get away from Omama until after 8 A. M. It rained and drizzled most of the morning, and from the soft character of the roads the going was very heavy and severe upon our men. We passed through immense fields of mulberry trees, as, also, large ones of wheat and barley. About mid-day we came upon the Tonegawa River—a rapid mountain stream—which we crossed on a bridge of boats, and thence across its dry bed to the town of Hongo, where we stopped for lunch, and here terminated our jinrickishaw journey, as we were now on the line of railway running from Tokio (Yeddo) to Takasake. After a good lunch, we parted with our faithful men, giving them a substantial *pour boire*, for which they were exceedingly grateful—acknowledging their appreciation by coming to our apartment and making repeated and profound bows—this being done while kneeling in our presence. One or two, I think, had already indulged in some " sake," and were more profuse than the others, but they were an excellent set of men, and I wish to do justice to faithful work.

At 3 P. M., we boarded the downward train, and at a point on the line I parted with my companions, they going to Tokio, while I continued to Yokohama, reaching there in time for dinner. Thus terminated one of the most agreeable and interesting excursions that I made in Japan—a trip that was most instructive in its character and furnished as much of beauty and varied interest as can be found, and in which I enjoyed the intelligent companionship of two as good fellows as are to be met in any part of the globe. This letter has grown to rather unusual length, but I could hardly make it less so and complete the excursion in a single epistle, which must be my excuse for consuming so much space.

XXIV.

YOKOHAMA AND ITS VICINITY.

GRAND HOTEL, YOKOHAMA, JAPAN.
(LAT. 35° 26′ N., LONG. 139° 39′ E.)
May 22d, 1886.

I HAVE made this city head-quarters during a good share of my stay in Japan, and from it made frequent excursions to interesting points in the interior. The city is very prettily situated on the bay, and immediately in front of it lies the shipping, which embraces representatives from nearly every nation. It is also a favorite rendezvous for our naval vessels, and as I write the war-ships *Omaha*, *Ossipee*, and *Alert* are at anchor within less than a half mile of the shore. A well-cared-for "bund" lines the water-front, and serves as an excellent lounging place and a good drive. The English and American ladies of Yokohama are usually good whips, and you generally find them holding the lines, even though there be a gentleman in the vehicle. Japanese ponies are cheap, and the cost of keeping one does not often exceed $20 per month, including the pay of the " betto," who fills the position of hostler, outrider, and outrunner. In the latter capacity he runs in advance of the team and clears the way. This is especially necessary when you drive through the rather narrow and crowded streets of the Japanese portion of the city.

Kanagawa, a mile or more up the coast, was the original port designated in the first treaty as the port of entry, but as the water was deeper and the harbor generally better on the Yokohama side, the former was soon deserted and the present site built upon. Our consuls are still accredited to Kanagawa, but their residence is in Yokohama, and one rarely hears the former place mentioned. I, however, paid it an afternoon visit, and wandered through a pretty Japanese garden, where there are some odd-shaped plants trained in various ways—a fancy in which the Japanese gardener delights. From the high ground in this deserted town one has a fine view of the bay, its shipping, and of Yokohama.

On the " bund," of which I have spoken, are located the hotels, the " Yokohama United Club," a few of the residences, and the agencies of the various steamship lines ; but the principal tea warehouses and establishments for firing the tea are on streets back of it, as are also some of the best shops for the sale of English goods and Japanese curios. It was the opening season of the tea trade during

GIRLS PICKING TEA. JAPAN.

my first day's stay in this city, and every one was exceedingly busy in looking after the early crop, which furnishes some of the best specimens of tea. The young shoots of the tea plant are the first gathered, and make the best teas, and it becomes a question both of pride and profit for the merchant to secure a share of this first picking. The tea, as sold by the Japanese grower or farmer, is not in a state that suits the taste or fancy of the foreign market; hence it is fired again under the supervision of Chinese experts. For this purpose large houses are constructed, containing long rows of open kettles, heated by small charcoal furnaces. Each kettle has its workman, or workwoman,—usually the latter,—and only a limited quantity is fired at a time. My impression is, that it takes less than a half hour to fire a given batch—the attendant stirring it all the while. I visited one or more of these establishments, and saw in one instance over three hundred hands employed in this firing process. Besides this, there were numerous other operations going on at the same time—such as assorting, mixing, and packing teas, and preparing the chests for shipment. So anxious are the merchants to get this new tea to market that the day of sailing of the *San Pablo* (one of the steamers of the Pacific Mail Line) was deferred two days that she might take the earliest product to the American market.

The best quality of Japanese tea comes from the

vicinity of the town of Uji and not far from Lake Biwa. It begins to reach the market about the 10th of May. The finest kinds are known as Sabo Mukashi and Gioku-ro, and these are sold at from $5.00 to $7.50 per pound.

The prettiest section of Yokohama, and where the largest merchants and wealthiest residents have their homes, is on " The Bluff," which is behind the city and elevated some two or three hundred feet above it. " The Bluff" consists of a long ridge, wider at some points than at others, and along it many pretty cottage homes are built. Each has quite a plot of ground attached, which is laid out in fine taste and ornamented by Japanese gardeners, who are celebrated for their skill and odd fancies in this species of landscape gardening. From the bluff you have a splendid view of the bay, and some of the residences command long stretches of water views, and in fine weather the great snow peak Fuji (the sacred mountain and pride of Japan) and its adjacent mountain ranges are in sight. In a short walk you reach, also, the race-track and a back bay, where bathing is excellent.

As you may imagine from the above, Yokohama is far from being an undesirable residence, and it is not at all surprising, when you put the question as to the length of their stay in Japan, to get the reply : " It is very uncertain." They have a temperate climate, a good market, and excellent society, so that, excepting the loved ones at home, they have but little else to ask for. It is quite different at most other places in the East, where every one is looking forward to the time of their return to their native land. My friends, Messrs. Elliott and N. Ferdinand Smith, two men from Smithtown, Suffolk County, L. I., have charming homes on " The Bluff," where I was made most welcome. In truth, I was urged to drop in at all times, and was assured that there was always a seat at the table for me. They are both fond of field sports, and in the shooting season bag their portion of game. On entering their grounds I was always greeted by one or more hunting dogs of the setter or pointer breed. I am glad to report that the firm they represent, Smith, Baker & Co., stands as well as any in Yokohama.

Of the excursions made in the vicinity of Yokohama that to Miyanoshita was among the very pleasant ones. It is something more than forty miles distant, and the route is along a well-travelled road, lined with villages. I had excellent company, and the trip was highly interesting. After passing Odawara, a town of considerable historic interest, the road begins ascending, and at the small village of Yumoto the carriage road stops, and from that point on you must walk or be taken in chairs or " kagoes," a species of palanquin that I could not stand, as in it the body is half doubled up ; so that I had a chair follow me, and used it in the steep parts of the road. Miyano-

shita is a favorite summer resort for the foreign population of Yokohama, and has a delightful summer
temperature.   There are two hotels, and that called
Fujiya is remarkably well kept, although the proprietor is a Japanese.   Yet he understands European
tastes, and his house is arranged for their comfort.
Even at this early season (May 3) I found some
travelling companions that I had met in China, who
were so pleased with the place that they were passing some time there.   There are numerous hot
springs in the neighborhood, and the water from
these is conducted through the town, so that you
have excellent hot baths at all hours.   There are
many picturesque walks in the vicinity, and one can
have a choice of several delightful ones.

The pretty little town of Kiga, situated in a very
narrow valley, and near which you have a fine view
of Fuji (Fusiyama of Europeans), furnishes a short
walk, and is a favorite one if you have an hour or
two only to spare.

The trip to Hakone and the lake on which it lies
is a longer one, and occupies some hours, but furnishes some grand scenery.   During the month of
May the sides of these mountains are clothed with
the beautiful pink azalea, which adds greatly to the
beauty of the scene.   I saw them afterward in
greater perfection about the mountains near Lake
Chiu-zen-ji, of which I have already spoken.   On our
return trip from Miyanoshita, which was made on

May 5, we had an excellent opportunity of observing one of the peculiar customs of Japan. It was what is called " Boys' day," and at every house where there had been a boy-baby born during the year there was a tall bamboo-pole, from which were flying one or more silk or paper fish. Some of these were very large, and, being of varied colors, the effect was pretty. The mouth of the fish is kept open by a small hoop, and the wind flowing in inflates the fish and gives it a remarkable resemblance to the live one. I counted at one house as many as seven fish on a single pole. I don't imagine these represented the number of boy-babies born to that house, but rather the joy of the parents, for in Japan, as elsewhere throughout the East, the male child is greatly prized over the female. Kite-flying was also indulged in on the 5th of May, and it seemed a general holiday. Old as well as young were engaged in this amusement, and at one village I counted over fifty large kites in the air at one time. These were of various patterns—some representing birds, others monsters, but the favorite form is rather rectangular-shaped. All were gaudily painted, and many had the cords so arranged as to produce musical sounds. Strange to say, I don't recollect seeing one of the bowed or kite shape—the one so popular with our boys.

The proximity of this city to Tokio (Yeddo), the Imperial capital, and the easy access by rail, enabled me to make frequent visits there. It is a very large city—having nearly 900,000 inhabitants—and bountifully supplied with water. A large river and numerous canals traverse it in various directions, thus facilitating the transportation of heavy products to different sections. Along these canals are the chief " godowns," or warehouses, where are stored most of the supplies. Even lumber is protected in this substantial way, and in case of fire there is sufficient on hand with which to begin building. I believe it is estimated that nearly all Japan is burned down once in ten years. No doubt some villages escape much longer, but the average life of a Japanese wooden house is about ten years.

There is much to be seen in Tokio, especially in the way of temples. Those about a section of the city called Shiba are large, and the grounds and walks are well kept. Here are buried several of the Shoguns, or military rulers of the country under the old *régime*, and their tombs are handsomely constructed. The bodies of others rest at Ueno, in another quarter of the city. This is a pretty part of Tokio, and is much frequented. There is a beautiful park, handsome tea gardens, and a race-course with a small lake in the centre—all within convenient distance of each other—and a museum, the richness of whose collection would compare favorably with that of many on the continent of Europe.

At a prominent point in the park the guide pointed

out two trees that were planted by General and Mrs. Grant during their visit to that city. One of these is a fir and the other a species of magnolia. Both are apparently doing well and seemed flourishing.

On one of my visits to this city I was treated to a native entertainment, where the " gesha," or dancing girls, contributed to our amusement. It began at an early hour (6 P. M.) and lasted till 11 P. M. The first part consisted of a feast, or dinner, largely made up of fish. rice, and sweets—all washed down by frequent cups of " sake," a light beverage made from rice, with about the same alcoholic strength as mild beer. The girls waited on us, and after the repast was finished, entertained us by a series of dances, or posturings, in which they introduced several figures. Fans were freely used, and the dance was very similar to that I've described in my letter from Kioto. After that we had some good juggling and legerdemain, and a ventriloquist gave us some good exhibits of his powers. Sometimes, I'm told, professional wrestlers form a part of such entertainments.

I was fortunate in one of my visits at Tokio (Yeddo) to get a peep at the Empress, who I learned intended visiting one of the handsome parks. By stationing myself along the route I heard she was coming, I caught just a glimpse of her. Her carriage was preceded by an officer in full uniform and an escort of lancers. Then followed the Queen in a light barouche, drawn by a pair of black horses of the country. The harness was trimmed in red and gold. There were two footmen and a valet, all in dark, tight-fitting clothes, trimmed in red and gold, and each wearing a gold cockade. The housing of the carriage was in blue, and handsomely ornamented. As the curtains were down, I only caught a passing glimpse of the Empress, who, with her attendant, was in Japanese costume ; but in the other carriage which followed were both ladies and gentlemen, all in European dress, showing that it is accepted at court. This change of dress is, I think, to be regretted, as the Japanese, being of small stature, do not appear as well in European costume as in their own flowing style of garments. The Mikado, when he attends the races at Yokohama, wears the European dress. His court or reception dress, I'm told, is a uniform with sword.

Social life in Yokohama I find very agreeable. The English mode of entertaining, with rather lengthy and set dinners, prevails. The ladies have their afternoon teas, and there are occasionally balls and evening parties. A large one, given by the "Yokohama United Club" just after my arrival, gave me a good opportunity of seeing the best element in social life. There have been some exhibitions of flowers that were well worth a visit. A fine collection of peonies, exhibited by a native gardener, was very attractive. I saw there the greatest variety and some of the most delicate colors, as well as the largest specimens, of this flower I have ever seen. The ladies of the city also held an exhibit of flowers in the principal hall of the town, which brought out a fine collection of flowers and plants, and showed some excellent designs for decorating dinner tables and some modes of training plants that were odd and interesting. Among the number was a pagoda, made up of growing ferns, that was beautiful in form and one of the prettiest things of the kind I've ever seen. The Japanese have a great fondness for training plants in odd shapes. They first dwarf them by cutting the tap-root—say of the pine or larch—leaving some of the minor roots, and then by tying the boughs in peculiar shapes, produce almost anything the fancy dictates. They grow them in a spiral form and various other designs. I've seen some very good imitations of birds— particularly the stork. The roofs of cottages and gateways are also imitated.

This must be my last letter from Japan, as I sail on the 25th inst., in the *Oceanic*, for San Francisco. In parting from this picturesque and very interesting country, as also from its polite, amiable, and apparently very happy people, I can't avoid expressing the feeling, which I believe is shared by most travellers, that this has proved one of the most interesting and attractive of all the lands I've visited in the course of this long journey.

XXV.

ACROSS THE PACIFIC OCEAN.

OCCIDENTAL & ORIENTAL S.S. "OCEANIC,"
NEARING SAN FRANCISCO, CAL.,
June 8th, 1886.

WHEN one has over 4,500 miles of water separating them from "the land where they
would be," a fair amount of caution suggests that
they select in time a good and comfortable ship in
which to cross it.   Such were my reflections when,
at the agency of the Pacific Mail, in Hong-Kong,
some months in advance of my contemplated crossing the Pacific Ocean, I requested the agent to
secure me a good stateroom (English cabin) on this
popular and well-fitted ship.   At best it is a long
journey and well tries the patience and resources of
those who have to take it, and therefore the voyage
should be made under the most favorable auspices.
A good and popular ship usually implies good
company and plenty of it.   The *Gaelic* and *Belgic*,
of the same line, are entirely new ships and beauti-

fully fitted with the addition of the electric light, but their dates for leaving Yokohama were rather later than suited my purposes ; hence I chose this vessel, and certainly have had no reason to regret it. She is the sister ship of the ill-fated *Atlantic*, which was lost, and with her so many lives, and was among the earliest vessels built by the White Star Line for the Atlantic trade. She has, however, been materially altered to suit the Pacific traffic, and has some fine large staterooms on the upper deck that are particularly light and airy and much sought for. Being among the earliest applicants, I was fortunate in securing one.

Our runs have not been very great—averaging about 290 miles in twenty-four hours—or, say, about 12 miles per hour—something faster than the steamers of the P. and O. service, but not quite up to the speed of the new *Gaelic* or *Belgic* of this line, and considerably slower than the trans-Atlantic steamers.

We have a fair number of passengers—some thirty in the first cabin, or saloon, a few Japanese in the second cabin, and over 800 Chinese in the steerage. Most of the latter are bound for San Francisco, and are returning under the last Chinese emigrant law—having been former residents of the United States. Why they will face the growing opposition in our country I can't well understand, but John Chinaman is a persistent fellow, and will take some

risks in order to accumulate money.   He shows his
force as an emigrant in the " Strait Settlements,"
especially in such cities as Penang and Singapore,
where he has monopolized many branches of industry.   You can't help respecting him for his manly
efforts, although you may not like Chinese as a body
or think them desirable citizens.

Of the cabin passengers some nine or ten, like
myself, are " round-the-world " travellers, or, as
they are frequently styled, " G. T.'s"—" Globe-Trot-
ters."   Some of these have been companions in
many of my excursions in the East, and encounter-
ing them again on this long voyage is like meeting
with old friends.   A share are officers of the India
Service, either civil or military, returning to England
via the United States, and a few are Hong-Kong
and China merchants that for variety are taking this
route home.   We have a few ladies to enliven the
whole, who materially assist in passing the long
hours on shipboard.   The days, having been particularly bright and sunny, have also been quiet ones,
so that exercise on deck has been practicable during
most of the voyage.   The track of our steamer, as
shown by the small chart exhibited in the companion-
way of the ship, and on which is recorded the daily
runs and a map of our courses, is interesting as
showing the advantages of " Great Circle " sailing, in
place of sailing what may be termed a direct line
from port to port.

An examination of the position of the ship, as given by her latitude and longitude, tells us that we started from Yokohama in latitude 35 degrees 26 minutes north and longitude 139 degrees 39 minutes east—only about two degrees south of San Francisco, where the latitude is 37 degrees and 49 minutes north, and that we have travelled northward on the arc of a curve as high as 48 degrees 26 minutes, or made quite 13 degrees of northing, and that we were over ten degrees to the northward of the place of destination. This apparent increase in distance is fully made up to us by the shortness of the degrees of longitude in the higher latitudes—being only about 48 geographical miles at the highest point ; and further, we were likely to get the favorable northwesterly winds which prevail at this season near the American continent, which in some degree we have done. The difference in distance in favor of the track we have followed over the one that would be made if we had sailed directly for San Francisco is about 300 miles, and in point of time about 24 hours.

If your readers will take the pains to follow our path on a globe, which they readily can from the record below, they will easily understand the force of the old saying (slightly altered) that "what seems the longest way round is actually the shortest way home."

Another feature of the voyage that was novel and interesting. and which can only be experienced by

the traveller who crosses the 180th meridian while
coming from the westward, is the gain in a day.
We passed that point on Tuesday, June 1st, and,
accordingly, the record shows two firsts of June and
two Tuesdays ; and as we sailed on Tuesday, May
25, we had three Tuesdays in nine days.   By making
the record thus, we entered San Francisco with our
calendars to correspond with those of that city, else
we should be a day in advance.   You may recall
that Jules Verne, in his *Tour du Monde en Quatre-
vingt Jours,*" makes a point of this, and the hero
really wins a wager, that he fancied he had lost, on his
ability to travel around the world in 80 days.   There
is another point to remark upon, and that is the
change of longitude from east to west, immediately
upon crossing the 180th meridian—this in order to
make it correspond with the charts, which are so
constructed—the longitude becoming west as soon
as you pass that point.   The following record of our
daily runs and the few incidents of the voyage may
not be particularly interesting reading ; still it serves
to show the " Great Circle " system of sailing, and
the dry details may be appreciated by those who
have made long voyages :

Record of voyage in O. & O. steamship *Oceanic*,
Captain Thompson, between Yokohama, Japan, and
San Francisco, Cal.   Distance, about 4,530 miles ;
average length of passage, 15 days ; left Yokohama
at 10.30 A. M. on Tuesday, May 25, 1886 :

Date, May, 1886.	Position at Noon.		Temperature.	Dis. since last rec.	Total.
	Lat. N.	Long. E.			
Wed. 26..	37.14	144.24	60	300	300
Thu. 27..	39.48	149.09	54	271	571
Fri. 28...	42.24	154.31	51	289	860
Sat. 29...	44.30	160.04	43	274	1134
Sun. 30...	46.17	166.40	41	300	1434
Mon. 31..	48.05	173.37	43	303	1737
June.	Lat. N.	Long. W.			
Tue. 1...	48.19	179.30	38	276	2013
Tue. 1...	48.26	172.43	38	270	2283
Wed. 2...	48.10	165.39	42	283	2566
Thu. 3...	47.47	158.15	42	298	2864
Fri. 4....	46.54	151.04	45	297	3161
Sat. 5....	45.34	143.54	49	310	3471
Sun. 6...	43.55	137.20	50	297	3768
Mon. 7...	41.51	131.21	58	291	4059
Tue. 8...	39.20	125.38	58	301	4360
Wed. 9...	Distance from San Francisco.....................				170

Total of ship's runs. 4,530

Remarks.—Yokohama's position by chart, latitude 35.26 north, longitude 139.39 east; position of San Francisco by chart, latitude 37.49 north, longitude 122.28 west. Remarks on state of weather, runs, etc.

May 25th.—Sailed from Yokohama; morning warm, and light clothing desirable; temperature about 70°. Many friends came on board to see us off; among those of mine were Gen. James H. Wilson, Lieut. T. Bailey, Myers, Mason, U. S. Navy, and Mr. Ferdinand Smith, of Smith, Baker & Co.

26th.—Bright, clear day, but cooler, and one felt like sitting in the sun; sea smooth.

27th.—Considerably cooler and overcoats necessary ; three blankets at night, day decidedly gray.

28th.—Morning cloudy and gray, but sun came out about mid-day ; sea still very calm. We passed, yesterday morning, immense streaks of the spawn of the porpoise and other fish ; it is of a dark reddish color, and often, the captain says, extends for miles. Many porpoises and whales in sight yesterday and to-day.

29th.—Weather dull and gray ; some rain ; coolest temperature since sailing from Yokohama.

30th.—Weather cooler ; wind fair since daylight, and most of sail set ; day rainy and disagreeable ; no Sunday services ; first omission since I left home in October last ; sea smooth.

31st.—Bad weather continued yesterday afternoon and into the night ; fog whistle began about 4 P. M. and continued till about midnight ; awoke with clear sky ; wind aft and fair, but rather too slight to be of much service.

June 1st.—Weather continued fine all the afternoon of yesterday, and the wind, though light. was favorable ; rather a heavy roll on and several seasick. Reached the highest point in the " Great Circle " sailing and crossed the 180th meridian ; the longitude now changes from east to west, and as we have gained a day, Tuesday, June 1, will be repeated to-morrow.

June 1st.—Wind still ahead and temperature low,

rendering it disagreeable on deck. Celebrated the event of two June 1's and two Tuesdays by treating all our table to champagne. As we sailed on Tuesday, we have had three in nine days.

2d.—Weather continues cold, but wind, although light, has been favorable and gives us hopes of a good run, which were partially realized. Sun came out, and brought many on deck, where they indulged in "shuffle quoits," etc.

3d.—Fine in afternoon ; somewhat foggy at night ; wind too light to assist us ; cold and raw ; sea calm, but considerable swell.

4th.—Sea has been calm for the past twenty-four hours, and yesterday afternoon was pleasant ; many up on deck playing " shuffle quoits ; " to-day foggy and misty and generally raw and unpleasant. Passed, about ten A. M., a sail, far away ; this is the first met since leaving.

5th.—Pleasant in afternoon of yesterday and night clear ; sails drew well all night and all of to-day ; considerably milder, but still cold enough for over-coats.

6th.—Wind fair during night, but light ; night clear and warmer ; sun rose beautifully clear this morning, and then it became cloudy. Services of Episcopal Church held in dining hall at 11 A. M.

7th.—Day all that could be wished ; beautiful, bright, clear, and mild ; no wind.

8th.—Day continued fine ; night beautifully starlight; wind sprung up about midnight from north-west, and we have been running at good speed ever since; will probably anchor about midnight in San Francisco Harbor.

9th.—Palace Hotel, San Francisco; arrived as anticipated; passed Custom House inspection without difficulty, and were at this comfortable hotel by 11 A. M.

The completion of this ocean voyage—the tenth since leaving New York City—virtually terminates my journey around the world, although our continent has still to be crossed before reaching the starting point; yet it is so well known that I shall hardly venture to keep up this journal in the detailed form that I have been doing. I may, however, if I visit places of special interest, send one or more letters.

XXVI.

VISITING THE YOSEMITE.

BARNARD'S HOTEL, YOSEMITE VALLEY, CAL.,
June 17th, 1886.

A TOUR around the world without visiting the Yosemite Valley would hardly be complete, especially in these days, when most travellers, and particularly those from foreign lands, are so full of it. They all know more or less of its attractions, and I'm free to confess that I learned more of the wonders and grandeur of this valley from my fellow-travellers abroad than I had ever before heard of. It seems to be one of the points that Europeans are bent upon visiting when they reach America.

Under such circumstances I could hardly do less than include it in my "run around the world," and the object of this letter is to give some of the impressions.

There are two principal routes to the great cañon of the Merced River—one by way of Stockton ; the other (called the Berenda) that takes you by way of

Raymond, Grant's, and the Mariposa Big Trees. Visiting the agencies of these routes in San Francisco entirely unprejudiced, and with the most honest intentions of finding out the best, you come away from each with a feeling that you are in greater perplexity as to choice than before you began your investigation. Each agent makes his so much the superior of the other that you wish you had avoided both and asked the first intelligent citizen you met on the street. Fortunately for me, I encountered a party that had determined upon the Berenda route, and as it was made up of fellow-travellers across the Pacific Ocean, I was not long in making up my mind to accept the proposition of joining them.

We made a party of six—just about the number to fill a coach without overcrowding—and as all proved most harmonious and entertaining, I take the liberty of adding their names : Mr. Cromie, of London, an old travelling companion of mine in a trip across the Atlantic in '83 ; Mr. Lind, of Scotland, long time representing the P. & O. Steamship Company ; Mr. Michaelson, of Bremen, of the firm of Melchers & Co., of Shanghai ; Mr. Townsend, of Manilla ; and Mr. Green, of a banking house in this city (San Francisco).

Leaving San Francisco by the 3.30 P.M. train, we crossed in a very comfortable ferry-boat to the opposite side of the bay, and in a large wooden station took a sleeper by the Southern Pacific Road.

The sail across San Francisco Bay—some twenty-five minutes—was interesting, and gave an admirable view of the shipping, the islands, and of San Francisco itself, the site of which is picturesque, but, owing to the irregular manner in which it is built, and the great variety of structures (mostly of wood), and these painted a dull gray color, it did not appear to me particularly pleasing. We started punctually, and in a few minutes reached Oakland, the Brooklyn of San Francisco. It is a pretty town and a favorite place of residence, as you escape the chilly winds which blow continually, during the summer, about San Francisco. Shortly after leaving Oakland we reached Berkley, a handsome village, situated on the slope of a high range of hills and with a southern exposure. Both it and Oakland have long avenues of trees—chiefly the *Eucalyptus Globulus*—which add greatly to their attractiveness. These trees are the growth of recent years, as the last time I saw Oakland it had only the low native live-oak, and those were not numerous.

The line of railway skirts along the shore of San Pablo Bay and the Straits of Carquinez, which connect it with Suisun Bay. We stopped for a few minutes at Port Costa, the narrowest point in the strait, and immediately opposite Benicia. At this place trains bound for the north and eastward are taken on a large transfer-boat, capable of holding nearly fifty cars, and crossed to Benicia. While the train stopped I had an opportunity of looking across the strait at Benicia, which I knew thirty-four years ago. Then it was a barren-looking spot, with scarcely a green thing to be seen. It now has quite dense foliage—so thick at some points as to hide many of the buildings of the town. Continuing our journey southward, the line leaves the border of the straits near Antioch, and then strikes across country through a rich agricultural and wheat-growing district. Most of the wheat had been gathered, but there were still some enormous fields where the grain was still standing, and which attracted the attention of my English travelling companions. Many of the farmers along the line were engaged in gathering their hay crop, which consists largely of oats, barley, and wheat, cut while in the milk and when the largest amount of nutriment is found in the stalk of the plant. This makes excellent feed, as the sleek coats of the California horses attest. Of course, the climate has something to do with the good condition of all animals on the Pacific Coast.

We stopped for supper at Lathrop, 95 miles from San Francisco; and if there is a meaner and less attractive station for refreshment than this, I hope I shall not encounter it. Berenda, 178 miles, was reached about half past eleven, when our car was detached from the train, and we passed the night on a side track—starting, early next morning, for Raymond, where we breakfasted and at once took a four-horse coach for Grant's, 22 miles away. The country passed over was rolling and at many points finely wooded with good specimens of the oak. Before reaching Grant's, where we dined, the country became almost mountainous, and we passed some quartz mining establishments.

Judge Grant, as he is known in this section—a man of over seventy-three years—came out to welcome us, and busied himself about our various needs—such as showing us the washroom, taking our hats, dusting us off—in fact, filling the position of both host and helper. He also assisted at table during dinner, and was ready to answer the numerous questions propounded by curious travellers. I am thus minute in my details concerning our host, as we learned afterwards that he was a man of large wealth—variously estimated at from a million upward—and had chosen this spot to end his days in—believing the climate of the country would add a few more years to his present three score and twelve. Some of my European friends were amazed when his history, and especially his large wealth, was told them, and were loath to credit it—remarking, as they became satisfied of the truth of his life, that "such an instance could only be found in America—never in Europe." The country from Grant's to Clark's (twelve miles) grew bolder, and some of the mountains we crossed were exceedingly abrupt; but as we were on a well-engineered road, our animals were not over-fatigued. Splendid specimens of pine and cedar, with some fir and oak, covered the country—many of the former rising over 200 feet.

We reached Clark's about 6 P. M., where we stopped for the night. In a small studio near the hotel we saw some well-painted views of the noted points in the Yosemite (Indian, " Large Grizzly Bear"), by Mr. Hill, an artist who ranks well in his mountain views. He was represented by his son, who received us very kindly, and also gave us some useful hints as to the best mode of seeing the most interesting points. He recommended that after our arrival and lunch on the following day, we take a drive through the valley and see the wondrous mountains from that level ; the next day visit Mirror Lake, Vernal and Nevada Falls ; and on the third day Glacier Point and Sentinel Dome. This order we followed, and after my experience I don't think any more comprehensive plan could be taken ; and in the course of these excursions you are repeatedly in view of the main valley and of the mountain peaks which border it, as well as numerous beautiful falls.

Our drive from Clark's to this hotel was over much the same character of country as on the previous afternoon—the road following along the south fork of the Merced River, and rising constantly till you reach the summit—6,700 feet. At Lookout Point we had a fine view of Signal Peak, the cañon of the

Merced, and distant valley of the San Joaquin. The country is heavily timbered with superb trees of the Coniferous family. The first glimpse we caught of the Yosemite Valley was a good one—El Capitan (7,000 feet) being directly in front. Beyond that were the Three Brothers (6,700), and in the farther distance North Dome (7,525), and Basket Dome (7,600). As we descended, other peaks became prominent, such as the Cathedral Spire (5,900), etc. At Artist's Point, directly on the stage road and some 5,000 feet above the sea, we had the most comprehensive view. It is a favorite one for taking a general view of the valley, and was named by Hill, the artist already spoken of.

After our descent to the level of ·this valley, we had a splendid drive of some three miles through famous forest trees to this hotel, passing *en route* that gem, the Maiden's Fall. It certainly is one of the prettiest that is to be found in this valley, and near sunset, when the sun shines directly upon it, is developed a superb rainbow that heightens its beauty.

We found comfortable rooms and fare at this hotel, which is the farthest up the valley and borders the Merced River. From its rear gallery one has a splendid view of the Yosemite Falls, the water of which takes its first leap of 1,600 feet, the second of 534, and the third of 500 feet, the view of the upper fall being especially fine from this hotel.

Our excursion to Mirror Lake and Vernal and Nevada Falls—all made in one day—was to me the most interesting of our trips about the valley. Making an early morning start, we were at the lake just in time to see the massive mountains which rise above it beautifully reflected from its surface. The foliage, too, which surrounds it, was equally distinct. After admiring it for a time, we mounted our ponies and travelled up the mountain side till near the Vernal Fall—a beautiful one of 350 feet, which comes down in a most graceful manner, and with its surroundings forms a beautiful picture. Continuing the ascent, we reached, by a circuitous route, the level of the fall, and near it, as if especially placed for our pleasure, nature has arranged a regular stone parapet, over which we looked down upon as beautiful a rainbow as I've ever beheld. After admiring it for a long time we continued on up the stream and stopped upon a graceful wooden bridge which crosses the river, where we lingered for some considerable time, admiring the grand rapids passing under us. The waters of these rapids are converted into the largest imaginable globules, the sunlight upon which gives them the effect of large, sparkling diamonds. A little beyond this is Snow's Hotel, where we halted for lunch.

The view of the Nevada Fall, which is only a short distance above the house, was to me a most impressive one, and I watched it from the piazza of an adjoining cottage with great interest and admiration. The waters, contracted into a narrow gorge, come rushing along to the brink of the precipice, when they suddenly take a fearful leap of 700 feet and are soon dissolved into a series of massive ridges of foamy whiteness, interspersed with numerous and beautiful shooting darts, greatly resembling in form, though not in color, the track made by meteors when shooting through the sky, and like them, too, they imperceptibly disappear as they descend through space. The entire surroundings are grand and ennobling. An enormous amphitheatre of towering granite rocks, among them the " Cap of Liberty " (7,060 feet), incloses the basin, into which the waters descend, and tall, graceful pines stand about as if admiring the scene and these wonderful works of nature.

The excursion to Glacier Point (7,200 feet) and Sentinel Dome (8,120 feet) proved a most interesting one and gave us beautiful and commanding views of the valley, its various water-falls, and the mountains which surround it. From Sentinel Dome you have a view of many of the peaks of the Sierra Nevada range—one over 13,000 feet in height.

To the lover of sport I would say that this locality furnishes a good field. Large strings of the rainbow trout are daily brought in by the Indians, who are good fishermen, and later in the season deer can be found in considerable numbers. In our excursion to the Nevada Fall I passed, on the trail, the tracks of two bears, which the guide said had been there that morning.

We leave here to-morrow morning—returning by the same route we came; but as we visit the Mariposa Grove of Big Trees after reaching Clark's, I'll keep this letter open, that I may tell something about these monsters of the forest.

PALACE HOTEL, SAN FRANCISCO,
June 20th, 1886.

Back again at this comfortable hotel, and right glad we were to reach it after two days of hot, dusty travelling. We arrived at Clark's on our return (26 miles) at 12 M., and after a hurried dinner were rushed off in the hottest part of the day to the Big Tree Grove, nine miles away, and not in a very good frame of mind to do justice to these stupendous monarchs of the Sierra Nevadas. However, that was not the fault of the trees, but of the stage agents and employees, who wish to consult their own convenience rather than the pleasure of travellers.

The big trees are certainly wonders, and grow upon one the longer they are examined. The following are the names and dimensions of a few that I observed : "Grizzly Giant," 72 feet in circumference and at least 200 feet in height; "Faithful Couple," 67 feet; and "Lafayette," 70 feet. A very tall, handsome specimen is named in honor of that great and good man, Abraham Lincoln. The poets Longfellow and Whittier are also remembered by two fine specimens standing near each other. The mountain road, which makes a circuit of the Big Tree Grove, passing near the finest specimens, is so constructed that it runs directly through one of these living monsters, and with our four-horse coach we drove through the one called "Wawona," halting just as the leaders reached the opposite side—the hind wheels being on a line with the side on which we had entered. This gave us probably one of the best and strongest proofs of their great dimensions, viz., a four-horse coach within the circumference of a standing and living tree.

This grove, like the Yosemite Valley, is now the property of the State—having been presented by the General Government under certain wise provisions—and each has a guardian who looks after them and assigns camping ground for those who wish to visit there in that manner. For the information of the visitor of the future to either of these interesting points, I will add that I've heard that the railroad company is pushing forward its line, and that probably within a year or two both will be reached with great ease and rapidity.